I0591333

THREE WISE MEN FOR CHRISTMAS

A HOLIDAY REVERSE HAREM ROMANCE

BRIE WILDS

RUTTISH
PRESS

Published by Ruttish Press, Sparta

eISBN: 978-1-63589-738-8
ISBN: 978-1-63589-751-7

Editor: Kasi Alexander
Cover Design: Brie Wilds

GET THE NEWSLETTER
Want to receive the latest information on my upcoming novels and receive a FREE book? Sign up for my free author newsletter by clicking on Brie Wilds Newsletter or visit www.briewilds.com

1

Claudia

Claudia Kraner killed the engine and stepped off the snowmobile. All around her was brightness. She'd endured it coming uphill, and now she cursed herself for forgetting her reflector sunglasses. When she'd picked up the vehicle from the garage about twenty minutes ago, the wall clock was just shy of 9:30 am. Despite being early, the sun was doing what it did best; it shimmered off the fresh powder that had fallen the night before. It would be great when she skied or snowboarded downhill.

Claudia felt the wind on her skin as it tugged at the fabric of her gear. She was well insulated, though without the Michelin man look. Well, Michelin woman in her case. Nicole her sister, had taught her that. Wear lots of layers of effective thermal gear that would trap small pockets of air between those layers. She'd done exactly that. A thermal polyester base. A down jacket for the mid-layer and a shell jacket as the top layer, which was way better than wearing one oversized chunky coat. She'd placed a cap over her head, holding her long blond hair in place, and had gloves, of course.

The surrounding glare was a total contrast to the dark storm that always found its way into her mind and soul at this time of the year. Right now, it was threatening to burst out of her. To help clear her mind, Claudia inhaled, filling her lungs with cold air, with the faint smell of burning wood. As a kid, that smell was a harbinger of Christmas, the forerunner of coming good times. She called it the Christmas smell. It used to be fun and exciting until that night, when everything changed and left a bitter taste in her mouth.

"Happy thoughts always," said Claudia out loud. She shook her upper body as if to physically shake off the imaginary shackles of darkness trying to consume her.

Claudia shielded her eyes with a hand to the forehead and surveyed her surroundings. In the distance, she saw the ski lift with the rest of the instructors and students coming up slowly. Not too far from where she stood, expert skiers went down Deer Edge Slope. It was one of the toughest at the resort, and their bodies twisted from side to side as they raced downhill.

Constant movement or throwing yourself into an activity could help you forget. Claudia hoped it would work for her too. That was why she was here today working, even though she should have taken the day off to celebrate. Since she was a kid, skiing, skating, anything to do with snow and ice had delighted her. From a young age, she had participated in skiing and skating contests and won more than a few. She'd skated in the few ponds scattered around their resort town and skied in the open space around their cottage.

Her sisters, Nicole and Holly, had not been as enthusiastic as she was about the outdoors back when they were kids.

Maybe because they were older and had other things occupying their minds. Her dad and mother...Oops, there she went again thinking of what she was trying to forget. She must find a better way. It's funny how the mind works. When you're trying to forget something, that's when you think of it all the more.

Claudia heard the whine and roar of a snowmobile and turned. It was her friend and fellow instructor, Jane Mackey, bringing the rest of the sleighs. Jane killed the engine and dismounted.

"Hey! Did you see the new instructor?"

Claudia nodded. Jane must have forgotten the engine of her vehicle was now turned off. She had seen the new instructor, and she had her sights set on him. She just hoped Jane didn't have the same idea. "Wyatt Webb, right?"

"That is what I call a hunk," said Jane. "I wish I could stare into those blue eyes forever."

"Why not?"

"Why not? Well, because I saw him checking you out. You could have him eating out of your hands." Jane snickered. "It could be a problem if this is the season Max finally acknowledges you."

"I think Wyatt is cute too. If I had a lasso, I would rope him in. As for Max, he's in a class of his own. Just likes to be admired from afar. I don't know. Maybe he thinks we're too young for him."

Jane placed a hand on her chest, then pointed at Claudia. "Twenty-two." And at herself. "Twenty-two, too young? Please. From what they say, men love younger women because the younger the girl, the tighter the vajayjay."

"It's not all about sex, Jane. Sometimes it's the conversations, the music, and topics one is interested in. They all play a part too."

"Well, I saw him eying you today too. Perhaps your day in the snow has finally come." She laughed at her own joke. "I wouldn't want to be you having to choose between two gorgeous men."

Claudia paused and looked at her friend. They'd known each other since their first year at Rutgers. She knew Jane wanted something. "Just two," said Claudia. "Flattery won't get you anywhere. Just tell me the favor you want, and if it's within my powers"—Claudia flexed her biceps—"I'll grant it. I'm in a favor granting mood."

"People grant wishes for special days. You're not married, and I know it's not your birthday."

Claudia felt a knot tighten in her stomach.

Jane's eyes sparkled. "It can't be your birthday? I remember back then at Rutgers, when we were freshmen, you said you were a leap year child. Anyway, I don't like the room they gave me. I'd prefer to be with the other instructors."

"You horny slut," said Claudia. "You have your eyes set on Wyatt. Proximity, right?"

Two red blotches appeared on Jane's cheeks. "No, it's the other instructor, Peter Malcolm." Jane looked down, and her voice faded as she spoke. "We had something going on last year."

"You dog. You're keeping secrets from me." Claudia pressed a gloved hand to her chest and shook her head in exaggerated disbelief. "You know what? Why don't we swap rooms?"

Jane's eyes widened. "Wait, are you serious?"

"Sure."

Jane ran forward and gave Claudia a hug. "Thank you." She rubbed a hand on Claudia's back. "And I mean what I said. You can have anything you want, but you'll have to wish on a shooting star."

"Yeah, right. Shooting star." Claudia looked up. "Okay, here they come back to work."

Jane stepped back and looked up. "Here comes your two hunks and the rest of our students. You better move fast. I can see the married women looking at Max and Wyatt with lust in their eyes. Make haste, Claudia. Go for Wyatt," Jane whispered.

"Why not Max?" Claudia replied in a whisper.

"He was in the army, right?"

"Mm-hmm."

"I overheard one of the older receptionists say he left his heart in the battlefield somewhere in the Middle East."

"He can leave his heart anywhere. All we need is his cock, right?" said Claudia with a shrug.

Jane rolled her eyes. "And I thought I was the hussy. Remember, Wyatt would fall like a stack of cards. I literally saw him undress you with his eyes."

Claudia shook her head and walked toward the approaching group. She felt her phone vibrate and heard the faint sound of an incoming text. She unzipped her outer jacket and opened the zipper of the breast pocket of her mid-layer. Inside was her phone in a transparent screen Ziploc bag. She looked through at her screen. It was a happy birthday wish from her sister Nicole.

Claudia felt like a vise had tightened around her chest. She struggled to breathe. Usually, she would have received Nicole's text early in the morning, while she was still in the privacy of her room. Something must have kept Nicole distracted. She always sent a birthday message first thing in the morning.

More birthday wishes would follow soon, Claudia knew.

She would have to find something to distract her. She searched for Wyatt in the group, but his face was turned away at an angle. Piercing blue eyes, square jaw, and a crooked smile that would melt the panties off any woman. It was better he chased her than vice versa. To give him the thrill of the hunt, so he wouldn't take her for granted. Or just not bite.

Getting rebuffed wouldn't be the end of the world. But with all the pain she was dealing with right now, it could set her down a path she had no control over. An experience she might not recover from. Just like she had no control over the day she'd come into the world, December eighth. She couldn't change the date her mother died, which also happened to be December eighth, fourteen years ago. Celebrating her birthday had always been double-edged. Time, they say, healed everything, but her wound was still raw after fourteen years.

2

Claudia

CLAUDIA'S HEART POUNDED LIKE A JACKHAMMER POKING holes in a frozen lake. She wanted to run and hide, but she had a job to do. If only her sisters would be more sensitive and realize that sending her a birthday wish was a constant reminder of a day she'd rather forget. Claudia knew it was more likely they were calling because even if everyone else forgot your birthday, your siblings never do.

Claudia's hands shook as she put the phone back in the breast pocket and zipped it up. She took a deep breath and as she exhaled, banished the thought from her mind as if expelling a ghost.

Jane locked eyes with Claudia. "Are you okay? Bad news?"

"No...no. Just a text from my sister...saying she loves me for no reason at all." It was a muddled-up truth. Claudia was surprised Jane had never pressed her on her birthday. On the other hand, why would anyone disagree with you about what you told them was your date of birth?

"Oh, one of those," said Jane. "I get them from my mom too. Then when I see her, she's so busy admonishing me for having a new boyfriend every few months. With that, she negates the affection her text had bought her."

Claudia nodded and looked at the people approaching them. The new students ranged from little kids to teenagers to folks in their sixties. They talked and laughed amongst themselves, with Matt Steel leading the way and Wyatt Webb bringing up the rear. It was just the second week of December, and Mountain Peak Skiing Resort (MPSR) already had a sizable group for their coaches to train for the week.

Mountain Peak, New Jersey, was a winter resort town, and people came from far and wide for their winter vacation and Christmas holiday. Usually, as it got closer to Christmas, the skiing classes would start to get larger as the town got inundated with vacationers. Claudia had been a volunteer in her preteens and began to work there every December once she turned sixteen.

"Students, please!" said one of the older administrators that came up with the group. He gestured with his raised hands for the others to come closer. He welcomed the students to MPSR and assured them they were in safe hands. He told them the history of the place and ended by saying that the most important thing was to have fun. The students gave him a round of applause. "Coaches! Let's put everything together for a run down the slope."

Claudia and the other instructors all came together and started to arrange the sleighs they'd brought up with snowmobiles.

"We're going to go down the slope on...on these sleighs?" asked one middle-aged looking man.

"Yes," said Max. His voice was deep and authoritative, like a man used to giving orders, and people following whether they liked to or not.

Claudia shifted her gaze to Max. He glared at the man that had asked the question with a look that dared him to say he wasn't going down the slope. Max was intimidating. Probably about six feet four inches tall, with an athletic build. His muscular legs and bulging arms were hidden behind all that insulating gear. Claudia knew because she'd seen him in the summers over the years without his shirt on.

Max was a guy to be obeyed. His skills at leading stemmed from being a graduate of West Point and having done a few tours in Iraq and Afghanistan, where he'd led men into dangerous situations. She knew he'd joined the army from high school and had come back to Mountain Peak after retiring from the military. He was an only child, and his parents had died while he was away.

Claudia came out of her reverie as Max started to direct people to sleighs. She felt her cell phone vibrate again and knew another birthday wish, or rather death day wish, had come in. Her mood darkened, then she remembered what she'd told herself earlier, to make herself happy. She glanced around, found Wyatt, and started walking toward him.

"Wyatt! Ride with Mrs. Robinson," barked Max.

Claudia stopped in her tracks. There was only one sleigh and two people left.

"Claudia, you ride with me."

Claudia could say no. She was under no obligation to follow his directions. Max was overseeing the instructors this year because he had volunteered to do so. None of the other instructors were obligated to follow his directions. Still, they all followed his lead simply because most people would follow someone who seems to know what they're doing.

"Okay, guys," said Max. "This is a gentle slope. Just to let you get a taste of what skiing is all about. I know most of you have played around in the snow before. Please just bear with us."

Since Max started working at the ski resort two years ago after retiring from the army, Claudia had been throwing herself at him. Well, not in the literal sense. She'd been infatuated with him since he and Nicole had been buddies in high school. She'd left enough clues that she would offer herself to him on a platter, but he never showed any interest apart from the typical day-to-day interactions when they worked beside each other. She didn't like him that much after that but didn't hate him either. Claudia remained frozen until she heard Max's voice again.

"Are you coming or not?" Max sounded indifferent, as if he didn't care if she came or not.

But Claudia felt her sex twitch. "Coming." she walked toward the sleigh. The thought that their bodies would be molded together as the sleigh went downhill sent a fluttery feeling to her stomach.

Claudia heard the fading mixture of screams of terror and joy as the sleigh of the other instructors and students flew down the slope. She couldn't believe Max was paying attention to her. Maybe Jane was right, after all. Claudia trembled as she sat on the sleigh.

Max sat behind her engulfing her with his smell, a clean fresh odor of men's body wash and a masculine spicy citrus smell of his cologne. His legs stretched out on either side of her. Her pussy twitched a second time. *Jesus!* He scooted forward and pressed himself flush against her. Soon something hard pushed against her butt. She didn't think it was his cell phone, but it could be.

He placed both of his strong hands flat against the snow

and pushed them forward. As the sleigh started to move and gather speed, Max grabbed Claudia's inner thighs for support.

Heart racing. A tingling sensation spreading all over her body, Claudia squealed as the sleigh took off downhill like a bullet. The air beat against her face and roared and whistled past her ears as they raced down. It tugged at her while Max's hands dug deeper into her thighs. In fact, they rested on her crotch. This was a pussy grab, thought Claudia. Jolts of pleasure shot through her sex and spread all over her body while the wind tore at her as if angry, trying to rip her head off her shoulders.

Claudia hardly had the strength to breathe. The force of the wind combined with the electrical sparks firing between her legs, caused by Max's hands working overtime on her crotch. It seemed like the devil himself had caught the sleigh with one claw, while the other was between Claudia's legs dragging her with a roar to hell. The more Max caressed her mound, the more her panties continued to flood. The combination of sexual tension and danger was rapture in a bottle.

In Claudia's mind, the surrounding snow melted into one furious speeding line as she felt an orgasm approaching. One moment she felt like she was coming, and the next, it felt like the sleigh would lose control, and she would perish. Everything was now in perfect harmony, and Claudia knew she was seconds away from the mother of all orgasms.

Without warning, the sleigh began to slow, the roar of the wind no longer a menace. The hands between her legs, seconds away from getting her undone, moved away from her crotch to her waist. It became easier to breathe again. At last, they were at the bottom. Climax denied.

Claudia was frustrated, and her mind a mess. She was more dead than alive. What just happened? The hard thing poking at her back went away as Max got up from the sleigh, extended a hand to her, and helped her up. She held his gaze, her eyes searching his, wondering if what she'd just experienced had really happened. Max had his poker face on.

"That was breathtaking," he said.

Claudia could hardly speak. She nodded, then tried to move, but her knees trembled, threatening to dump her on the snow.

Max walked away, talking to other students and making sure they were okay.

Claudia looked up to the slope they'd just descended, the sun reflecting off it like a mirror. Maybe she should drag Max up for another run? Claudia knew she would never look at a slope normally again.

Did he really do that? The question kept on going back and forth in Claudia's mind. She looked at Max again, and but it seemed like he had moved on, not interested in finishing what he'd started.

Claudia took a few deep breaths, regained her composure, and searched around for Wyatt. She saw him helping some people with Jane. Needing to keep her mind busy, she headed toward them.

3

Claudia

CLAUDIA CHANGED DIRECTION AS MAX HEADED TOWARD Wyatt. She stopped, ran her hands across her jacket as if she were looking for something while keeping an eye on the duo.

Claudia knew something had happened on that slope. Whether Max's hands being where they'd been happened to be intentional or not, Claudia knew she'd damn near come on those slopes, and an impending orgasm came to a screeching halt through no fault of hers. Now she was *horngry*, horny, and angry.

From the corner of her eye, she saw Jane walk away from Max and Wyatt. Max always got straight to the point. Now, she had firsthand experience. He'd just grabbed her pussy. She wasn't complaining, but why didn't he take the bait she'd been dropping all along with her body language? Right now, she just needed someone to help her forget the hurt of December eighth.

The students gathered, according to who they came with, each one reliving their experience of flying down the slope. Soon, they would leave with other coaches to begin their instructions.

Claudia's phone vibrated again. She bet it was another meaningful text from a family member. The dark mood she'd momentarily forgotten threatened to return. No, she wouldn't let it happen.

She looked at the slope they'd just came down and remembered the snowmobiles. "Shit," she said under her breath. They had to go back up and get them. She heard the crunching of footsteps in the snow as some one approached, but she continued to look up the slope.

"Hi, you're Claudia Kraner, right?" said a deep rich voice behind Claudia.

She spun around, and her mood brightened. It was Wyatt. "Yes."

"I'm Wyatt Webb, one of the new instructors. I saw you win a skating tournament many years ago in Vermont."

Heat traveled down Claudia's back. As a kid, she spent a lot of time outdoors, and once she started walking, she was on skis and skates. Anything that moved fast. "Well, I'm Claudia, as you already know. Competitive ice skating was a long time ago."

"Yes, same for me. Mine was skiing, though. The last time I skied competitively was in college. The only time I get to ski nowadays is during the season like now. I take a job as an instructor, just like this one. A change of pace from my regular job as a computer analyst."

Claudia nodded. "How do you like Mountain Peak so far?"

"It's nice. As good as popular, better known skiing places.

If you live in the Tristate area, you don't have to travel far to Vermont or Colorado to ski." Wyatt looked up the slope.

Claudia stole a look at him and liked what she saw.

"I saw you looking up the slope. I guess you're thinking about the snowmobile, how to get them back." He looked at Claudia, and their eyes lingered. "I can help."

Claudia felt his eyes searching and probing inside her soul until he found a tender spot to hang on to. A tingling sensation ran through her body. "Okay." She should tell Jane not to worry. That Wyatt would bring back her snowmobile. Then she saw Jane walking up the slope with her man beside her. The one she wanted to get closer to by swapping rooms with Claudia.

"Do you want to walk or use the lift?" asked Wyatt.

Claudia said walk so they could talk as they went up and make a connection. But the wind had changed direction and now came down their way. It snatched the words from their lips. At the top of the hill, they retrieved the vehicles, and Wyatt rode behind Claudia. It was not the same as the sleigh ride, but that was on her mind as they drove down to the garage where the snowmobile and other snow machines were kept.

As they left the garage, they passed a skating pond. A few people were already on it. Wyatt gazed at it for a minute.

"I know you'd rather be indoors keeping warm, but do you think you can spare like twenty minutes to teach me some moves?"

Claudia tapped a finger on her lips. "What's on your schedule?"

Wyatt looked at his watch. "I have a snowboarding class in ten minutes, followed by two more."

"It's just like mine. You know what. Meet me back here

when you're done, and I'll show you whatever you want to see."

"Really?" Wyatt winked. "And I'll show you mine too."

Claudia's nostrils flared. She pulled at her collar.

"Just messing with you," said Wyatt quickly. "Deal." He started to walk away, then turned. "See you soon."

Claudia watched him walk away and shook her head smiling, then she went to get things ready for her class.

After each lesson, Claudia would walk to the lounge. It served two purposes: having a cup of hot chocolate and getting out of the cold. Time flies when you're having fun, and before Claudia knew it, Wyatt was back.

"Okay, ice queen, turn me into an ice skater," he said as he put on his skates.

For the first five to ten minutes, Claudia showed him how to maintain his balance and move. He was too clingy. He was always dragging them down and soon they were giggling like teenagers on the ice. Claudia became suspicious.

"How long have you been skating?" asked Claudia.

"Why do you ask?"

"Because I've seen people who can't maintain their balance fall. And I've also noticed people who have a careful way of slipping and falling."

Wyatt grinned. "And which group do I belong to?"

Claudia smiled. "You tell me."

"What I can tell you is that I feel like I've known you for ages."

Claudia was on thin ice, with Wyatt over her. "Same here." He had already invaded her personal space. He leaned forward and brushed his lips against hers.

"What're you doing later tonight?"

Claudia almost said it was her birthday and she was going to celebrate. But she stopped. "Why do you ask?"

"Once I'm done with the gym, my calendar is kind of open, and I was wondering if we could go out later tonight. Get a bite to eat and have a few drinks."

"Okay, sounds like a plan."

4

Max

MAX STEEL WAS ANGRY WITH HIMSELF. HE SAT IN THE SKI
resort lounge, sipping coffee and hating himself. He was the
only one in the lounge for now. It usually came alive at night
when the bar was open. Guests of the resort could come in for
a drink, listen to music, watch TV, or just hang out. As it got
closer to Christmas, it would fill to capacity like any other bar
in town. But it was quiet at this time of the day. Dead as how
Max felt inside.

Why didn't he respond when Claudia had looked at him
with those inquiring round eyes last season? He could have
sealed the deal then. Max had seen the hunger and the want in
her eyes. All he needed to do was ask her if she wanted to
grab coffee, and the rest would take care of itself.

Claudia was no fool. She must have felt his fingers on her
crotch even though he hadn't meant to grab her. The speed of
the sleigh had surprised him when he launched the sleigh, and
that was the only way he could get a firm grip and not fall off.

He'd buried his nose in her hair, and his groin was flush against her backside as the sleigh shot down the slope. Even now, the smell of her hair, a mixture of vanilla and wildflowers, still clung on him. If he were a betting man, he would put money down that she'd backed into him and enjoyed his hands on her as much as he did.

Two years ago, after he'd left the army following the accident—he was so happy to see her when he applied for the job as a ski instructor. She was all grown from the last time he'd seen her. Now, she had flat abs and curves where it mattered, ass, butt, with well-defined arms and legs. All that skiing paid off. Being in the army, joining Special Ops had taught him a lot and also taken a lot from him.

Max and the Kraners had attended the same elementary and high schools, just like every other kid in Mountain Peak. Nicole Kraner had been his classmate in high school, and her little sister Claudia he remembered, was more interested in boys activities. She would go fishing, play football, baseball, and soccer, instead of hanging out with girls playing with dolls or just gossiping.

Max had forgotten about her until he came back from the army. Now she was all grown up, and he could have a relationship with her without it seeming like he was robbing the cradle. All he needed to do was make a move. Today he'd made a move, but he didn't think it was the right move. He could have followed up. Maybe apologized and then asked her out.

Max heard a burst of laughter drift in from outside. Out of curiosity, he walked to the window to see what was going on. People were skating, and a couple was on the ground, fooling around. Then he realized who they were, and his whole body went rigid. He watched them get up and start to skate again.

Claudia was skating with that asshole Webb. And he was

doing a great deal of falling. And to Max's annoyance, Claudia was sucking it all up. She was trying to pull him up, but he kept jerking her hand to join him on the ice.

Webb seemed to think he was the next best thing to German bratwurst sausages. But he was just another asshole with a pretty face and pecs bought from a gym. He wouldn't have lasted a day in Iraq or Afghanistan.

Don't hate, Max Steel, he admonished himself. *The US army today was an all-volunteer force. You volunteered; Webb chose not to.*

Max's thoughts drifted back to Claudia. If he hadn't just blown her off, that would have been him frolicking around with her. Touching her, holding her, and speaking sweet nothings into her ear. He was a fool for letting his past define him. He should leave the past where it belonged and focus on the present and the future.

Max knew he should make his move soon. Nothing would hurt him more if he finally made his move, and she said, "Max, I was waiting for you to ask me. If only you'd asked me first."

His chest heaved up and down. "Jesus," he said in a low voice. He was so mad he could see himself getting hold of Webb, opening an artery, and watching him bleed to death.

5

Claudia

THE NUMBER OF HAPPY THOUGHTS GOING THROUGH Claudia's mind negated all unhappy thoughts that threatened to pull her day down.

Once she finished the private lessons with Wyatt, they parted ways and agreed to meet at 7 pm in the lounge. Claudia went to her room, packed her stuff, and headed to Jane's room to keep her part of the bargain.

Jane's hands shot to her chest once she opened her door. "Oh my God." Claudia stood there, suitcase in hand. "I didn't know you were serious."

"Well, I am. Grab your things and get out of here." Claudia went in, sat on the bed, and looked around. The room was no different from hers. A closet, bathroom, a queen-sized bed, a TV, and a couch. What else would a girl want?

Claudia glanced at the couch and wondered how many times someone had been fucked on it. If only hotel room furniture could talk.

"You're glowing. Happy? What's the secret?"

Claudia smiled. "Nothing."

"It can't be nothing," said Jane, casting Claudia a wide-eyed look. "We were roommates for a good part of three years. I know that look. Either you've been laid, or you're looking forward to getting some dick."

Claudia grinned, then bit her lower lip. "Nothing serious. Just going out later this evening with Wyatt."

"Aha," said Jane as she walked around the room, picking up her stuff. Her shoes, a jacket, then she unplugged her phone charger from the wall. "I told you he was all wound up for you." When Jane finished picking up her stuff and was ready to leave, she looked at Claudia. "Are you sure you want to do this? Because with something developing between you and Wyatt, you don't have to travel far to get to his room, nor him to yours."

Claudia grinned. "Well, you must have heard of this song. *Ain't no mountain high enough to stop me from getting to you.*"

"Okay, I get it. Have fun."

"Now get out of here before I change my mind."

Jane left and closed the door behind her.

Claudia smiled and hoped she would have a good outing with Wyatt. Now the question of whether to tell him about December eighth or not came up again in her mind. She decided not to. Let sleeping dogs lie.

Where should they go? Hawks Lair was always an option. They could go to the bar in the hotel at the mall. Have a drink, and then visit the German Christmas Market. If Wyatt hadn't been there before, he would definitely like it.

She wouldn't mind going there again, either. She loved the spicy sausages with potato wedges, fried onions, and bell peppers. Another exciting place would be the place of mists.

Claudia giggled. That would be moving too fast. Skinny dipping in the middle of winter? Not everybody's cup of tea. But she had a feeling Wyatt would like it.

Moreover, she didn't want to visit everywhere in one swoop. Save some for later. When the time was right, they would go up the mountain to the place of mist.

She opened her suitcase, brought out her toiletry bag, and headed for the bathroom—time to get ready.

6

WYATT GOT OUT OF THE SHOWER AND TOWELED HIMSELF DRY. He stood in front of the mirrored closet door to retrieve his clothes. Broad shoulders, bulging biceps, and awesome six-pack abs stared back at him. He'd kept in shape by skiing and lifting weights when he could. He couldn't help admiring his body. Any physical attribute Wyatt had he credited to his mother. Wyatt hadn't known his father. His mother told him that the bastard had walked out on them when he was just eight weeks old. His father's excuse was that he wanted to focus on his career, and a crying baby wasn't going to help. He'd promised to come back, but he forgot to say when. That was thirty years ago.

His mother worked two jobs and sometimes three to make ends meet and give him the education that finally led to a business degree and a career as a stockbroker. His now almost sixty-year-old mother decided the winter of New York wasn't ideal for her anymore. She'd found a job in Florida and relocated. Wyatt visited her whenever he could during major holidays and vacations.

He still couldn't believe how things had progressed so far. Claudia Kraner was a dream come true. He hadn't been lying when he said he'd met her many years ago at the skating ceremony. Wyatt had been about twenty-two then and had gone to the skating tournament with a friend. He'd seen her compete in a contest. She'd been tall and lanky, just becoming a woman.

Her intense concentration and focus on the competition had drawn him to her. He'd kept an eye on her to see how she would do in the competition, and she did well. He was impressed by her demeanor and filed her name away in his head, and that was it. Over the years, he would remember her and wonder what she was up to.

When not spending the winter vacation visiting his mom in Florida, he would travel to Europe to ski. Wyatt had heard about Mountain Peak from a colleague at work and was checking it out when he saw a picture that triggered his subconscious. It was the girl from the skating competition many years ago. Now she was all grown and one of the instructors at the ski resort at Mountain Peak.

Wyatt couldn't believe it when he saw an opening for an instructor and knew he had to be there. He had won one of his alma mater's three championship trophies, and being a champion would be an advantage when he applied for the job. And here he was.

Wyatt had always believed that marriage was for suckers. It had nearly ruined his mother, and he didn't think it was natural for a man to tie himself down to one woman. Wyatt avoided commitment like the plague, always moving on when the girl he was dating wanted more. But since meeting Claudia, all kinds of new thoughts had invaded his mind. The few hours he'd spent with her were a dream come true. One thing he was sure of now that he'd found her, he wasn't letting her go.

Wyatt settled on a pair of faded jeans, a white shirt, and a black T-shirt, and brought them out of the closet. He didn't want to be too aggressive with his pursuit of her, nor did he want to chase her away by making her think she can't measure up to him. He planned to play it by ear.

With Claudia, he knew he had competition too. He'd seen how Max Steel looked at her. Wyatt had googled him. War hero, good looking with an incredible physique. Wyatt would have liked him, but he saw the hunger in his eyes when he looked at Claudia. He probably had the upper hand too, since he'd known her for a longer time.

Wyatt chose his cologne carefully. He wanted something memorable, an emotional trigger. Something she would always connect to him once she smelled it. He settled for an aromatic, woody blend of patchouli, citrus, rosemary, lavender, and other flowers, put together by Giorgio Armani.

Satisfied with his appearance, Wyatt headed for the lounge with a black lightweight winter jacket draped over his arm. He passed a couple on the way and turned halfway after to see that they'd both done a double-take. Wyatt smiled. If his looks didn't do it, then the cologne would.

Once he stepped into the lounge, Wyatt did a quick scan, but there was no Claudia yet. He didn't think she would have changed her mind. The lounge was half full. A few people glanced at him when he walked in, then went back to their conversations and drinking. He stood beside the bar, eyes glued to the flat-screen TV mounted on the wall. It was almost 7 pm, and he prayed his fears wouldn't be realized. About five minutes later, a silence descended, as if someone had shushed the room.

Wyatt swung around and froze. Standing by the door, her frown changing to a smile when she saw him, was Claudia. Fresh-faced like a baby, with her hair in a ponytail, wearing an off-white sweater blouse and a pair of faded blue jeans, Claudia was a sight for sore eyes. Conversations around him resumed, but his heart continued to pound in his chest.

Wyatt's eyes drifted to her suede fuck me boots and then back to her face.

"Sorry I'm late," said Claudia walking with a funny gait towards him. She laughed, looking down at the boots. "I'm awkward in heels. It was a gift from my sister, Holly. I've always been a tomboy. Heels and dresses are not my thing. I'll go with pants and flats any day."

"Hey, I don't blame you. I'm awkward in them too."

Claudia laughed and punched him playfully on the shoulder. "You don't wear heels."

"For the record, you are beautiful."

Claudia smiled and raised her hands. "Stop it. Stop it." Nodding her head and still saying *stop it, stop it*, she motioned with her hands for him to continue.

Wyatt narrowed his eyes. "Wait." He cocked his head and wagged a finger at her. "Are you urging me on, and at the same time saying stop the flattery?"

"Yep. I see you pay attention to details."

Wyatt threw his head back and laughed. "You are funny. Shall we?"

They put on their coats and headed outside.

7

WYATT

WYATT PUSHED THE KEYLESS ENTRY FOR HIS BMW X6. THE car's lights flashed. "This way." He opened the door for Claudia.

"Wow, nice car."

Wyatt's eyebrows shot up. "Are you into cars?"

"No, but I can see it's nice."

Wyatt chuckled, shut the door, and walked to the driver's side.

"So where are we going?"

Wyatt started the car, backed out of the parking space, and headed for the road. "What do you think of the German Christmas Market?"

Claudia gave him a thumbs-up. "My choice too. They have the best sausages."

The German Market wasn't exactly what Wyatt expected when they arrived. There were rows of tables on the side-walks, but they were mostly empty. A few families with little kids walked around. An open stall sold gingerbread man cookies and pretzels. The smell of baked goods and something spicy hung in the air.

Claudia found the source of the spicy aroma, and soon they were seated in a restaurant enjoying plates of bratwurst, potatoes, onions, and bell peppers.

Wyatt took a long drink from his mug of German brew to chase down some of his sausage and potatoes. He put down his glass and looked at Claudia across from him. "So it gets busier than this?"

"Pfft! Of course. Today, December eighth is what I call a case of *you ain't seen nothing yet*." Claudia waved a fork speared with a piece of sausage in front of her, then put it in her mouth.

"What do you mean?"

She raised a finger as she chewed.

Wyatt had expected her to say today was her birthday when she mentioned December eighth, but she didn't. Did he have the date right? He'd seen her profile on the ice-skating website.

Claudia swallowed. "By next week, the place will be completely full. You'll see men walking around in traditional German garb, and women dressed like pretty fräuleins. All types of German delicacies will be on full display, served and eaten in boatloads. A large Christmas tree will be lit, with Christmas carols performed in English and German. And of course, Santa will be at hand to offer presents."

"Maybe we'll come back then, too," said Wyatt, and added with a smile, "I'd like to sit on Santa's lap."

Laughter bubbled out of Claudia. "You'd probably break his legs and get a lot of kids angry. And they'll launch snowballs at you." She gave him a once-over. "With a white beard,

Santa's belly suit and costume, you'd make a handsome Santa replacement. I'll sit on your lap."

Wyatt's cock twitched. *Let it go, cowboy. You don't want to appear to have a one-track mind.* Moreover, Claudia was on her second glass of German beer. That could have loosened her up.

"So you work at the resort every season?" asked Wyatt.

"Yes, since I was a teenager. Even my sisters worked there too. Before I turned sixteen, I would volunteer for an hour or so. Skiing is one thing most kids around here know how to do. When I turned sixteen, my dad let me work full time during the season. I just love snow. What about you? Why did you decide to coach at MPSR?" asked Claudia.

I've been infatuated by you since I saw you at that skating competition. But Wyatt did not say that. *To get to know you better.* Instead, Wyatt said, "Found out about the resort from a colleague of mine, a fellow stockbroker on Wall Street. It was a way for me to kill three birds with one stone. It was like getting paid to ski and have fun."

Claudia looked at him, eyes narrowed. "That's two birds. What's the third?"

Wyatt felt this was an excellent segue to the truth. "Spending time with you."

Two red dots appeared on Claudia's cheeks. She lowered her eyes. "But you just met me."

"Not really. Remember the skating tourney at Vermont Township many years ago? You won first place."

Claudia's eyes brightened. "Seven years ago! You were there?"

Wyatt smiled and nodded.

A corner of Claudia's lip crinkled in a smile. She dropped her hands on her lap, shaking her head. "No way."

"Yes way." Wyatt described what she wore and the things

that happened. "A friend of mine had dragged me there. Skiing was my thing, not skating."

Claudia couldn't remember a lot of what he described, but it sounded familiar. "Wow, those were the days. I don't do competitive skating anymore."

"Same here. Well, skiing. My last competition was winning one of the three skiing championship trophies my alma mater has."

They ate on in silence. Claudia wiped her mouth and placed the napkin on the table. "Did you like it? I mean the sausages."

"Yes, very good. Definitely will be back. Dessert?"

"No."

"Maybe later?" asked Wyatt.

Claudia nodded.

"Good." Wyatt signaled for the check.

Claudia grabbed her handbag and brought out her wallet, just as the waiter arrived with the bill.

"Don't worry, I'll take care of it," said Wyatt.

"Nope. Why don't I meet you halfway?"

"No."

"I insist."

Wyatt looked around as if expecting someone to rescue him. He stroked his chin, then snapped his fingers. "Why don't I take care of it this time, and next time, it will be your turn?"

Claudia looked at him with lips pouted, then nodded. "Smart, securing a second date while the first one wasn't over yet."

Wyatt smiled. "You're giving me too much credit." He settled the bill, and they left.

They drove past their MPSR accommodation, and Claudia turned to him.

"Where are we going?"

"There's a place called Hawks Lair. It's a restaurant bar and grill and sounds interesting. I thought we'd check it out too."

Claudia shook her head slowly and rubbed her stomach.

"I know you're stuffed. We'll just hang out by the bar or get a table and have a few drinks, and I'll tell you a new story."

"You'll tell me a story?"

Wyatt smiled and nodded. They were now driving past Main Street with the decorated streets and stores lit up with Christmas lights. They headed for the mountain road, directed by the GPS.

"Shut off the GPS, and I'll show you the way. Keep on driving uphill. When you see a sign that says Hawks Lair, turn into it."

Wyatt parked the car, walked over to the passenger side, and let Claudia out.

Wyatt had called earlier to make a reservation for two. Once he mentioned his name, the hostess looked through a clipboard with a list, then ushered them to a table for two, lit up with candles.

"Aww, I love candles," said Claudia.

Wyatt pulled out a chair for her.

She looked at him and smiled. "Thank you. You'll make someone a good husband one day."

Wyatt chuckled and took the other seat. He looked around, taking in his surroundings. They had an oval-shaped bar, with the bartender in the middle, and the half-occupied bar stools looked like skiing enthusiasts huddled around their coach.

The sound of conversations and utensils being used drifted

mixed with the soft Christmas music being played in the background. On little tables like theirs scattered around the restaurant, the few that were occupied had couples like them too. The booths had families with children. Wyatt remembered Claudia's remark about making someone a good husband and smiled.

One wall was lined with black and white photographs of what Wyatt thought were the local school's sports teams. Another had pictures of famous people who had visited the restaurant in the past, old photos of hunters and people skiing. Hawks Lair had a rustic vibe to it.

The hostess handed a menu to Claudia, then Wyatt. She lingered when giving Wyatt his menu.

"Let me know if I can be of service to you," she said in a low sexy voice, batted her eyes, and walked away.

"Let me know if I can be of service to you," said Claudia, mimicking the girl when she was out of earshot. "Women, so disrespectful."

Wyatt pretended to bury his face in the menu. He didn't want to be included in that discussion. Moments later, he asked, "Are you ready to order?"

"No, I'm still full. I'll just have a cocktail."

Wyatt offered her the wine and cocktail list.

Claudia looked through. "I'll have a daiquiri."

A woman dressed in a black top and pants walked up to their table. "Hello." She gave Claudia a Pan Am smile and turned to Wyatt, and her whole face lit up. "Hi! I'm April. I'm your waitress for the evening. Are you ready to order?"

Wyatt smiled back. "Hello. The lady will have a daiquiri, and I will have a Manhattan."

"Okay," said the waitress, and collected the menu. "I'll be right back with your drinks."

Wyatt made a tent with his fingers and focused on Claudia. "So will you be celebrating Christmas with your family here in Mountain Peak?"

"It depends. Dad moved to Florida about a year or so ago. I don't know yet if he's coming. At least Nicole will be here. They have a huge vacation home here. Holly, maybe. She-"

"There you go." The waitress put down Claudia's cocktail.

Claudia picked it up. "Thank you." She took a long drink.

"Thirsty, eh?" said Wyatt, taking his.

"Can I have another one?" blurted Claudia just before the waitress left.

She nodded.

Wyatt raised his glass. "To friendship." He clinked glasses with Claudia and took a sip.

"To friendship." Claudia took a sip and put her glass down. "What about you? You'll be here until the end of the season?"

"I'll be here for Christmas. I would have gone to Florida, but I was there for Thanksgiving, and moreover, Mom is spending Christmas with her friends on a cruise. I have to be back in the office after the new year."

"I'll definitely be here," said Claudia.

They talked about movies and books, and when there was a lull in the conversation, Wyatt said, "What about that dessert? Up to it now?"

"Sure, I'll have some ice cream. Vanilla if they have it."

Wyatt raised his hand for the waitress. "We'd like some dessert, please," he told her. "Vanilla ice cream and coffee for me. Do you have any chocolate cake?"

The waitress raised an eyebrow. "Triple-chocolate melt-down okay?"

Claudia pouted her lips. "That sounds decadent."

Wyatt winked at the waiter. "Perfect."

"I'll be back with your order."

Wyatt leaned forward. "I'll let you sample mine if you'll let me taste yours."

Claudia leaned forward. "I've been waiting for that. Show me yours, and I'll show you mine."

Wyatt hadn't expected that. "We're still talking about ice cream and cake, right?"

Claudia smiled, her eyes on him as she took a sip. "You tell me."

Wyatt looked over Claudia's shoulder and saw their waitress coming back. Behind her were five others. In her hand was a big chocolate cake with a candle burning in the middle. They surrounded the table and started to sing.

"Happy birthday, happy birthday!
Today you can have your cake and eat it too.
Happy birthday!"

The singing was off-key and terrible, but Wyatt beamed. The surprise was perfect.

Claudia's mouth dropped open. Her eyes were so wide they looked as if they were going to pop out of their sockets.

The waiters were not done. They continued at the top of their lungs.

"Are you one? Are you two?"

Claudia's nostrils flared. Her lips quivered.

"Are you three?"

Claudia got out of her chair and ran for the exit.

8

Claudia

CLAUDIA RAN TO THE EXIT AND STEPPED OUT, THE COLD enveloping her. It felt like stepping into a skating ring dressed in nothing but a leotard before a contest. She stopped. A lifetime of skating and skiing, being outside in the snow had conditioned her somewhat to the cold. But it had also been drummed into her by coaches too, to never expose herself to the elements unnecessarily.

Why did he have to order a cake? The night had started so well, and now he'd gone and muddied it all up. But it wasn't his fault. He didn't know. In fact, most people didn't know. It was December eighth, fourteen years ago. A cold day just like this one.

It was Claudia's eighth birthday. Her mother had baked her a cake and decorated it with her favorite colors. Still, she'd also wanted eight unicorn candles on the cake. Mother hadn't found them in the local store and forgot to check on online.

Claudia threw a tantrum when she came back from school and there was no unicorn on her cake. Their mother called around, and a novelty store in the next town had it. She left Nicole in charge of her and Holly got in her Subaru and drove off. Claudia remembered waiting and waiting for her mother to come home until she started to worry that maybe her mother had run away from home because she, Claudia, was too demanding.

Sometimes, Claudia, too, had felt like running away. She'd stuff her backpack with toys, but there was nowhere to go to.

After some time, Claudia just wanted her mother to come home and forget about the unicorn candles. She never did.

Later that night, a sheriff's deputy drove up to their house. There had been an accident. A semi-trailer had run a red light and smashed into a blue Subaru they thought belonged to Mrs. Kraner. They needed her father to come with them to identify her body. Claudia had sent their mother to her death. Approaching footsteps drew her out of her reminisces.

Claudia smelled him first before she was sure it was Wyatt. A surge of adrenaline had released his musk. It mixed with his cologne, and a small fire was lit inside her. She felt an arm around her shoulder and looked at Wyatt through a cloudy haze.

"Really sorry, I didn't mean to upset you."

Claudia knew he hadn't. It wasn't his fault. He just didn't know.

"Do you want us to leave?" He rubbed her shoulder. "Come on, let's get our jackets."

A tear trickled down one cheek as Claudia saw the hostess coming with a man who she presumed to be the manager from his purposeful steps.

"Hi. I'm Roger the manager. Everything okay?" His eyes darted from Wyatt to Claudia and back to Wyatt. "Is she okay? Was it something we did?"

Claudia turned to look at them. "I'm sorry, Roger. It's okay. I got…too emotional with the birthday singing."

The manager exhaled, the relief on his face as clear as the champagne flutes in the bar.

"Well, if there's any way we can be of assistance, please do let us know." He smiled, nodded, and walked away with the hostess.

"I need a drink." Claudia headed back toward their table, and Wyatt followed.

"Sorry I upset you," said Wyatt. "I didn't mean to-"

"No," said Claudia. She tossed her drink down her throat. "You didn't know."

"Is it something you want to talk about? Sometimes when you talk about things, it might help you better deal with it."

Claudia shrugged. "Maybe." Back then, she and her sisters had been evaluated by doctors and were found to be okay. "It's my birthday, and I haven't celebrated in a long time with anybody. I'm going to drink, but I'd appreciate it if you didn't so you can get us home in one piece."

Wyatt signaled for the waiter, and after her drink came, he focused on Claudia as she told her story.

"There you have it. That's why I never celebrate my birthday. You're the first person that has ever taken the initiative and dragged the truth out."

Wyatt took Claudia's hands in his. "It wasn't your fault. It was an accident. You must forgive yourself and let go. You did what kids do, and your mother did what mothers do."

The way Wyatt stared into Claudia's eyes like his gaze had the strength to lift her out of how she felt took her back to the little fire that had lit inside her. She felt something for him, even though she'd just met him. "Can we go back to MPSR now?"

"Sure." Wyatt called for the bill, settled it, and left a generous tip.

They drove back with Christmas songs playing in the background from the radio.

"It's beautiful out here," said Wyatt, looking out of the window at the snow-covered forest landscape.

"Yes, but I don't really see it anymore. When you've been in a place for so long, you don't see the beauty anymore. You have to leave and come back. Only then can you see with new eyes to appreciate again."

"Wow, that's deep. And it applies to anything in life."

Wyatt drove to their building and opened the door with his own key. "I'll walk you to your room."

They were almost by her door when she remembered she'd swapped rooms with Jane. "Oh, God. So sorry. Jane and I exchanged rooms just before I came out to meet you." She gestured with her thumb. "That way."

Wyatt smiled. "Let's go."

Meeting Wyatt this morning, going skating with him and then having dinner had all led up to this moment. He'd done the research and arranged for her to have a cake to celebrate her birthday. He did that because he cared. He'd cared since he saw her at the skating competition. Was that infatuation? Or latent love? Could he claim he was now in love after meeting her for a few hours? In love, after a few hours? In romance books, they call it insta love. She stopped at the door. "This is me."

"Oh, all right. I wish the night would never end."

"This is my best birthday since I was seven, thank you."

Wyatt shrugged. "So is life. I hope I'll be there to spend more birthdays with you."

Claudia giggled. "That sounds like a marriage proposal."

"We'll call it a night then. Are you all right?"

In reply, Claudia stepped into his space, raised her lips, and brushed them against Wyatt's. At first, he didn't respond, then he took her lips hungrily, pushing his tongue into her mouth. Wyatt backed away, breathing hard.

"It's not right," he said. "It's like taking advantage of you. You had a few to drink-your emotions are..."

"I'm fine. A little tipsy, but I don't care. Come in." Wasn't that sick? Her libido was roaring with her panties all wet on the anniversary of her mother's death.

Wyatt backed away. "I'll see you tomorrow, okay?"

"Okay," said Claudia, her voice a whisper. She slid the key in the hole, but she didn't want to be alone. She didn't want to end the night with Wyatt feeling sorry for her. He'd waited a lifetime to get his hands on her, and he was backing away. She turned and looked at him with puppy eyes. "Please, Wyatt, I don't want to be alone. Once I fall asleep, you can leave."

Wyatt swallowed. "Okay."

Wyatt's voice was tight, and Claudia knew he wanted her too. Right now, she didn't need anybody to be sorry for her. All she needed was someone to fuck her.

9

Claudia

WHEN YOU STRIKE A MATCH, IT BURSTS INTO FLAMES. THAT was what happened between Claudia and Wyatt once they were inside her room. She brushed up against him, and the fuse was lit for an explosion.

Wyatt's finger traced down her body hungrily. It demonstrated he knew what he was doing, and he'd done it a million times with other women. But right now, she just didn't care. She was horny and in pain. And Wyatt fucking her would ease it.

His mouth hovered over hers, his lips brushing and retreating, causing Claudia to open her mouth and lick her lips in anticipation. This seemed to go on for eternity. For the first time in her life, Claudia grabbed a guy by the neck and forced his mouth against hers.

An animal-like groan escaped from Wyatt. His hot tongue parted her lips and drove into her willing mouth.

Claudia moaned as her legs turned to jelly. Even though

she was damaged, the cause of her mother's death, his action showed he wanted her - fault, blame, and all.

His hot lips continued to plunder her mouth, and she shivered against him. When his fingers at last began to explore her body, she let him. They roamed over her, exploring her curves and squeezing, setting fires all over her body. It felt like striking one match and using it to light eight candles.

Claudia unbuttoned her sweater blouse and flung it away. Wyatt paused for a second, stepping back from her lips and looking at her breasts barely contained by her bra.

"Jesus." He breathed and buried his face between them.

His fingers went behind her and made quick work of her bra clasp. Her breasts tumbled out, and she heard a sharp intake of breath from Wyatt. He lowered his head on one nipple, wrapped his lips around it, and started to suck.

Claudia threw her head back as his wet lips on her nipples sent jolts of electricity all over her body. Her swollen sex twitched, ready to receive. Her thigh muscles clenched and unclenched, doing the Samba.

Claudia's mind was running a mile a minute. She'd slept with only two guys: the guy who had taken her V card in her first year at college, and her boyfriend for the rest of her time at Rutgers, a British guy who had run back to his country after graduating. They'd been classmates, both graduated with a degree in economics. It was more a relationship of convenience and proximity. Claudia was so excited. She'd never done anything like this before.

Wyatt seemed like he loved to take charge, and he was now in control. His fingers were unforgiving. Stroking, pinching, and sliding.

Claudia liked to give as well as she got, but this was so damn good her legs were trembling. She couldn't hold herself up anymore as Wyatt focused on her breast as if he were hypnotized. He took turns sucking each nipple, sending floods of pleasure all the way down to her girly bits.

Anticipating that her legs would give way sooner rather than later, Claudia inched back, a hand stretched out behind her, hoping to make contact with the bed. When she did, she eased her back onto it.

Still latched on to her tits, Wyatt followed.

Claudia lay back on her elbows and watched him feeding on her beasts, fascinated. For a second, with the way he was going at her boobs, she wondered if he was getting some nourishment from them.

His fingers stroked and caressed, taking her to new heights. Her last sexual experiences paled next to what Wyatt achieved with his fingers. Claudia could only imagine what the main course would feel like and hoped she didn't have to wait long.

Wyatt traced a finger down her tight stomach toward the tip of her panties. He added another finger, and both easily slipped underneath the fabric toward her mound. They continued down to check how wet she was. Claudia's pussy was flooded.

Wyatt pulled his hands out.

Claudia watched him as he brought his glistening fingers up and slipped them into his mouth.

He closed his eyes and sucked on his fingers. "Sweet."

When he opened his eyes, they were fiery blue.

He unbuttoned and took off his shirt, grabbing the bottom of his T-shirt and slipped it over his head, exposing six-pack abs, broad shoulders, and bulging biceps.

"Let me know if you want me to continue," he said, his words rushed. His chest rising and falling as if he'd run a mile. His muscles were alert, body poised, ready to take action.

Claudia's heart beat as if it was going to burst out of her chest. *You just met this guy, and you're going to let him fuck you?* The answer was yes. But all she managed was a whimper. Not to cause any confusion, she reached for his waist and started to unbuckle his belt.

Wyatt let her go at it while his hands went for her two free mounds of quivering flesh again.

Claudia knew that different men loved different parts of the female anatomy. Wyatt was unquestionably a breast man. He looked at them greedily, then grabbed both with his hands.

He took a nipple in his mouth, tugged and nibbled, then bit down.

"Oh God," gasped Claudia and lifted her rib cage from the bed. Sweet pain, like a bolt of lightning, exploded from her nipples and traveled all over her body. She didn't want him to stop.

Wyatt dragged his tongue down her stomach, leaving behind a wet trail and quivering abs. He hooked his thumbs to the side of her jeans, pulled them down to her ankles, and tossed them to the side.

Claudia's eyes never left his face as he did the same with her panties and flung them. They landed with a wet thud.

Wyatt spread her legs, planted a kiss on her inner thigh, then sucked on it.

Claudia gasped as an electric charge shot straight to her core, causing her toes to curl and her thighs to quiver.

Wyatt continued, taking his time running his tongue in circles on the skin of her inner thighs, nibbling, and biting. Then he changed direction and slowly traced a part toward her swollen sex.

Claudia was a quivering mass. Her breathing came in gasps. The small fire burning inside her was now turning into a raging inferno.

Wyatt was taking his sweet time. A painter and connoisseur rolled into one. He was a pussy...her pussy aficionado, doing his best work and admiring it all at once.

Each time Claudia reached down to rub her clit and bring an end to the sweet torture, Wyatt knocked her hand away.

Then he placed his mouth on her core, and all hell broke loose.

Her hands shot out and grabbed his head as his hot mouth spread her lips, his tongue darting in and out of her center. Claudia turned her head and buried it into the pillow. An exhilarated moan escaped her lips, urged on by the animal-like grunts from Wyatt.

Her ex-boyfriend had only gone down on her reluctantly with a few pathetic licks, but Wyatt was a master. His tongue set her ablaze. All the cylinders in her mind were firing, leaving no room for her to think about her birthday, her mother's death, and her sisters sending her constant reminders. In fact, she was thrashing around, devoid of any thought.

"Easy, girl," said Wyatt as if calming an out of control kitten. His breath was hot against her pussy, and the vibration of the mumbled words caused her sex to throb and flood anew.

"Your boyfriend never liked the taste of pussy?"

Before she could process the question, Wyatt slipped a finger inside her, then a second one. Claudia's whole body trembled, and she immediately forgot what she was thinking about in the first place.

Claudia was full of heat, even though it had snowed earlier, and the ponds outside were frozen solid. Sweat glistened on her body, and Wyatt's forehead was dotted with the stuff too.

Claudia's clit was hard and engorged like a little dick. Wyatt wrapped his lips on it and rolled his tongue over and over the knob, causing tsunamis to radiate from her pussy all over her body. As if that was not enough, he sucked on it, drawing guttural moans from her.

At the same time, Wyatt was finger-fucking her. Deep, hard, and fast. She loved the sensation delivered by the unfamiliar shape of his fingers inside her like a bolt of lightning shooting electric currents straight to her brain, delivering jolt after jolt of pleasure. Her muscles clenched around his fingers, and she let out a quivering breath from her open mouth. "Oh God." She loved it all. It felt so good.

"Wyatt, I want you inside me." Claudia's voice was so tight she barely got the words out.

Wyatt replied, sounding completely breathless. "Okay." His voice was tight.

Claudia heard him finish unbuckling his pants, the same ones she'd abandoned when he started…doing things to her. Claudia tried to get on her elbows, to examine his cock, but her body was so shaky she collapsed back on the bed.

Wyatt tapped his cock against her mound, making a wet, heavy sound.

Claudia felt his warm body settle between her legs and gasped when he slipped into her, stretching her and filling her up. She'd only fucked two cocks in her twenty-two years, and this, the third, was almost six months after her last fuck. Wyatt was so long and thick that each time he slid back into her, she felt a tingle like the very first time.

Wyatt's blue eyes stared into Claudia's. "Baby, you feel just as sweet as you taste."

Wyatt was big, much bigger than her last boyfriend. With his palms on the bed, he'd propped himself up with both hands beside her, his cock sliding slowly in and out. He closed his eyes, lifted his head, and turned it from side to side. "This feels like heaven."

Claudia wanted to shout, to sing. She grabbed her breasts and squeezed them. The sensation was out of this world. She threw her head back, her fingers digging into the sheets.

Wyatt stared to piston into her, sliding in and out.

Claudia felt he was punishing her for sending her mother on an errand she never came back from. For denying her sisters their mother, and her father a wife. She deserved to be punished. She squeezed her thighs and wrapped them around Wyatt to get him to slow down. To prolong her punishment. His eyes were ice blue. Like he was looking but not seeing. He fucked her hard as he sought an angle for maximum sensation.

Without warning, Wyatt slowed to a crawl. "This is so good," he breathed. "I don't want to come yet."

"No," she said with a whimper. She looked at Wyatt with pleading eyes. She deserved to be punished for what she'd caused her family. She just wanted him to fuck her. She squeezed her muscles around his cock to get him going.

Wyatt jerked and threw his head back. "Fuck." He blew air out through his mouth. "Baby…baby, please don't do that again. I can't hold it if you continue to do that."

Claudia bent her knees, giving him more access. "Fuck me."

"Oh God," said Wyatt in a shaky voice. "You have no idea what words like that do to me." A deep grunt exploded from his throat. He leaned forward and placed his weight on her, her nipples scraping his chest. He reached down and cupped her ass cheeks. His hips opened at full throttle, resuming the piston-like precision.

His weight on her drove her breath away, but it felt so good. Claudia moaned. "Deeper, harder, faster." She embraced the intense rush of pleasure she felt she didn't deserve.

Claudia watched more dots of sweat appear and coalesce on Wyatt's forehead. They dripped down his face, neck, and onto his chest. They both were slick with sweat. He continued to drive into her, fucking her until she was a throbbing, sweaty mess.

The *phlu phlu phlu* sound of a hard cock entering a wet soaking pussy filled the room.

"Oh my God," said Wyatt. His body went rigid, and he started to shake.

Claudia felt him get bigger inside her. And when he came, his fingers dug into her ass cheeks, pulling her into him. His whole response dragged Claudia to the top of the mountain and triggered her own climax. It started with a pulsating feeling deep down in her pussy. Her whole body shuddered uncontrollably like a volcanic eruption was taking place deep inside her. She let out a scream, unable to move, think, or speak, shivering and whimpering under Wyatt.

10

Claudia

CLAUDIA PUT AWAY THE SKIS THE GROUP SHE TRAINED HAD rented, then drove over to the garage to park the snowmobile. Next, find Wyatt. That is, if he didn't come looking for her first. Right now, she wanted to take a bath. It had been a long, sweaty day.

It had been four days since Wyatt had given Claudia the surprise of her life at Hawks Lair and then fucked her brains out. Since then, they'd been together when they were not working. What she had for Wyatt was more than what she had ever felt for the last two guys she'd dated. Was it love? Time would tell.

Claudia knew from being around Wyatt, and the way women were attracted to him, he wasn't the committing type. Her plan was to take it one day at a time.

Claudia had been blindsided by Wyatt's gesture at Hawks Lair. In the past, her family soft-pedaled around the issue of her birthday. They would wish her a happy birthday, then wait for her to take the lead and decide what should happen, which always ended up being nothing.

But Wyatt had taken the lead. Even though he didn't know there was a history to the date. That eighth of December was totally different from what she was accustomed to. He'd ripped off the bandage and reopened the wound, and she'd basically relived the day again. The smell of freshly baked cakes and cookies had pervaded her nostrils. Her anger when the candles she wanted were not there, and her relief when her mother decided to go find them. The anxiety and despair when she finally knew her mother was dead.

Claudia was ashamed her response had been released as sexual tension, but she was glad Wyatt had been there. He also made her realize that there was nothing she could do about it. It was all in the past. She couldn't go back in time and change things. She could only make the best of it, and beating herself up wouldn't help matters.

He had awakened something in her, a desire to be alive. To participate in what was going on around her, and not just be a wallflower. She looked up and saw Jane coming toward her and smiled. Now there was someone living life to the fullest.

Jane smiled. "Hi, Claudia." She leaned closer to Jane. "I still can't believe you slept with Wyatt the first time you were left alone with him. I had no idea there was a little whore in you."

Claudia looked down, the back of her neck heating up. "I didn't know either." She looked up at Jane. "I guess you rubbed off on me."

"Ouch," said Jane and raised her hand for a fist bump.

"So when are you leaving?" Jane's guy had invited her on

a road trip to New Hampshire. Just the two of them to visit some of his friends for a few days.

"Right now. Just came to say goodbye. I'm going to miss you."

"But you're coming back, right? And you have your phone?"

"Yeah."

Claudia grinned. "So that's no big deal. With a phone, it's like you never left. We'll be in constant contact."

A car tooted its horn.

"That's me," said Jane. She came over and hugged Claudia. "You stink of exhaust fumes. The snowmobile, right?"

Claudia lowered her head to her shoulders and sniffed. "Yeah, I know. I'm taking a shower and getting out of these once I'm done here."

Jane started walking away, stopped, and turned. "I think you're in trouble."

"How?"

"Max is going to make his move on you soon. I guess now he sees you spending time with Wyatt - it's his kick - in - the - butt -. Let me know what happens, okay?"

Claudia laughed it off. "Nothing is going to happen. Max doesn't care for me like that."

The horn sounded again.

Jane ran off. "Later."

Claudia remembered the sleigh ride with Max. *Hmm, or does he?* It was his action on the sleigh that had made her so horny on her birthday. Max Steel basically made the bed, and some other person had slept in it. She waved at her friend and then headed for the lounge. She would pop in and then head to their quarters to take a shower. What Jane had said crossed her mind again. She laughed and dismissed it.

Claudia rounded the corner and saw Max and Wyatt

standing together talking. Seeing the people she was thinking about caused her footsteps to falter, almost stopping. They both looked up when she approached. Max's face had been stern, but now it softened.

Wyatt had been frowning. Now he smiled and waved. "Over here, Claudia."

Claudia liked that Wyatt didn't call her Claud or shower her with attention in public.

"Hi, Max. Hey, Wyatt. What's going on?"

They both said hi in unison.

"We were just talking about the scheduling," said Max. "We're a bit short on instructors, only for a short while, though."

"Oh, I didn't even think of that," said Claudia. "Jane and her guy."

"We hope to bring in some new people too. We have two new students coming in today. I was-"

"I can take them both, I don't mind," said Wyatt cutting Max off. "We don't have to overload Claudia's schedule."

"No, I don't mind," said Claudia. "I can-"

"You heard the man," said Max. He glared at Wyatt but was talking to Claudia.

Claudia sensed the tension and wondered what else was going on. She clapped her hands. "Okay then, I'll see you guys later."

Claudia left them and headed for her room, wondering if there was anything else causing tension between the men. Back in her room, she turned on the shower to get the hot water going, then took off her clothes and threw them in the laundry bin. She took a shower, put on clothes similar to the ones she'd had on before but clean, and headed back to the lounge.

A car pulled up at the accommodation quarters as she passed, and a man and woman exited.

Wyatt must have seen Claudia from inside the lounge because he soon appeared at the door.

"Hey. You're back. I saw you from the window."

"Yes, I just needed to take a shower. Is there beef between you two? There seemed to be some sort of tension."

Wyatt shrugged. "Nothing really. Just guys flexing their muscles."

"Hello. Excuse me," said a voice.

Claudia turned to see the man and woman who had gotten out of the car. The woman was talking to them.

"Wyatt?" The woman's eyes narrowed. She got more confident. "Wyatt Webb!" She looked at the man with her. "It's Wyatt Webb."

11

Claudia

THE GIRL WAS BLOND, TALL, AND PRETTY. PROBABLY IN THE same age range as Holly or Nicole. A little wind blew snow from the roof of the lounge, which felt like she was being pelted with small grains of sand. It also brought a familiar smell that Claudia believed was the girl's perfume. It wasn't the usual flowery smell, but something rich and powerful. Claudia didn't care a lot about scents, but she'd sampled Chanel No 5 once at the mall and what she smelled now was just like it.

The girl was dressed all in white as if she was doing a photoshoot in the snow. Claudia's eyes moved from the excited blonde to the man she was with. Square jawed, black hair, wearing jeans, a sweater, and a down jacket, he too had an amused look on his face, as if he were used to the girl getting excited suddenly.

Claudia's eyes drifted back to Wyatt, who had an embarrassed look on his face like he'd been caught with his hand in the cookie jar.

Wyatt brushed invisible hair away from his forehead and grinned. "Hello, that's me."

"I knew it!" the girl squealed. She ran toward him and threw herself at him in the name of a hug. Then she stepped back and looked him over again. "It was my second year at New York University (NYU), and I watched you win gold at the skiing event in upstate New York. Look at you!" She turned to Claudia and spoke to her as if she and Claudia were old girlfriends. "Most times—well, for me—when I meet people I've been crushing on in real life, they don't measure up, but he still looks amazing! Oh God, sorry. I got too excited and forgot my manners. I'm Riley, Riley Carter, and I'm here to learn all about skiing and do some photoshoots in the area."

"Wyatt Webb," said Wyatt, smiling. "I'm one of the seasonal instructors." He pointed at Claudia. "Claudia Kraner. She's an instructor too."

"Hi," said Claudia with a smile and a nod.

"Oh, my photographer," said Riley, pointing at the man she came with. "Cameron Dawn."

"Nice meeting you," said Cameron, smiling and nodding his head, first at Claudia and then at Wyatt.

Claudia smiled back. *If I were him, I wouldn't be happy if the girl I came with is jumping all over another guy.* His gaze lingered on Wyatt as if he were giving him a warning. A look that said *You better keep your hands to yourself even though Ms. Riley here has the hots for you.* Claudia noticed Wyatt had crossed his hands over his chest, with a *Bring it on* smirk on his face. *Jesus,* thought Claudia, poor Cameron is feeling insecure, and Wyatt wasn't helping. Claudia's head jerked to Riley when what she'd just said registered in her head.

"You're going to be my instructor, right?" said Riley in a flirty voice. "I don't think I'll be comfortable with any other instructor."

Claudia knew that Wyatt had already volunteered to take on the new people, but leaving Wyatt with Riley would be like asking a hungry person to watch the pantry.

"All the instructors here are good. Any of us will have you racing downhill in no time."

"Yes, I know," said Riley, "but you're the only state champion. Gosh, I hope this will be the beginning of a new phase in my life."

Wyatt had no comeback to that.

Just like that it was settled, and Wyatt became Riley's coach. Wyatt directed them to the admin building to register and get accommodation.

Once they left, Wyatt and Claudia left for his room. Claudia didn't think it was right to ask Wyatt if there was anything between him and Riley. She'd been there when they arrived. She'd seen the whole thing unfold. They made love, he showered, they made love again, and they ordered some Chinese food. Claudia slept like a baby in Wyatt's arms. Skiing and sex in the same twenty-four hours was a lot of work.

The next morning, they were back to the usual grind. Just before Claudia left to climb onto the ski lift, she saw Riley already hanging on to Wyatt like a messenger bag. Cameron was there too, snapping pictures of Riley. Right now, she was glad Wyatt had agreed to take on Riley and Cameron.

Claudia met with her team for the day. They got on the lift and went up to the slopes. She worked with several groups. She had lunch, and when she was done for the day later in the afternoon, she saw Wyatt still instructing Riley.

"No way," said Claudia to herself. They were at the

skating rink, and after a few minutes of watching, it would seem like Riley wanted more than just being instructed on skating. *Well, don't jump to conclusions.*

Claudia went closer to the pond so that at least Wyatt would see her and wrap it up for the day. At this point, she was beginning to get irritated with Riley. Riley was hogging his time for herself. Since she'd been there watching, Riley had fallen to the ground five times, and each time begged Wyatt to help her up. Claudia was sure Wyatt had seen through her ruse and was fed up with her. But each time she faked a fall, he ran up to her like a dog playing fetch.

Claudia turned to the sound of footsteps crunching snow. It was Cameron. *Now something is going to go down.* "Hi, Cameron."

"Hello, Claudia. Please, call me Ron."

"Okay." Claudia smiled apologetically. There was this boyish quality about him that drew her to him. "But mine is still Claudia, though."

Ron laughed. "That's fine."

Just then, Wyatt looked her way and waved. "Hey."

Claudia waved back.

Wyatt skated to over where she was with Ron. "Hi, buddy!"

Ron nodded his hello and moved away.

"Are you almost done? I'm famished."

Wyatt sighed. "I think you'll have to go ahead without me. Riley wants to spend as much time as possible learning." He shrugged as if it was out of his hands. "She's one of those people that learn faster with a fire hose approach to learning. I'll come and find you as soon as we're done, okay?" Wyatt pecked her on the cheek and skated back to Riley.

Claudia stood there, staring at them, wondering what to do. It seemed like they were just skating. Wyatt was only doing what he did best and what he'd signed up for. Riley was getting her money's worth.

"Riley's really enthusiastic about skating and skiing," said Ron as he walked back to Claudia.

Claudia peered at him. Couldn't he see that his girlfriend might cease to be his girlfriend if things were not checked?

"She's taking it seriously."

"I can see that. Anyway, I'll talk to you later. I have a few things to take care of." Claudia knew she had no right to be angry, and she tried not to be. She was just pissed off. With her and Wyatt, there was no us. Their relationship was undefined. Only two people that liked each other having fun. By the end of the month, everybody would go their separate ways.

Claudia found herself at the entrance to the lounge. She yanked the door open and entered. The smell of coffee, food, and wood fire greeted her. With more people coming to the resort as winter vacation started to gather steam, it was profitable for them to serve food now.

She took off her gloves, stuffed them in her pocket, and rubbed her hands together. Claudia sat on the barstool. It was the same bartender that had been there since when she was below the drinking limit.

"Hey, Claudia. What can I get you?" he asked. "I know you like hot chocolate, but have you tried Irish coffee with whiskey?"

Claudia made a face.

"You've clocked off, right?"

She nodded.

"Just coffee with a little kick."

"Okay, why not."

The coffee whiskey mix was good. Tasted a lot like Irish cream to Claudia, but it was hot. She blew at it, then sipped and looked around. A few people she knew were sitting down over a meal and talking. It would be dark soon, and she hoped that would be enough reason for Wyatt to say enough is enough for one day to demanding Riley. There was the flood-light too, and people could skate the whole night if they wanted to.

When her coffee was half gone, Claudia went over to the window and looked. Wyatt and Riley were still there. Ron had gone. At this rate, Wyatt would be exhausted by the time he got out.

Baffled by Wyatt's action, Claudia exhaled noisily. She turned and saw Max Steel sitting on a chair close to the fire-place. He looked so calm and handsome. She remembered what Jane had said and wondered why he'd never made a move on her. Well, maybe this was the time to find out. Claudia took another sip of her coffee and headed toward him.

12

WYATT

WYATT HAD NO IDEA CLAUDIA'S MOTHER HAD DIED ON HER birthday and the story behind it. Would he have moved forward with that birthday cake gesture at Hawks Lair if he knew? Probably not. At the end of the day, he was happy he hadn't known. He would never make her unhappy unknowingly, but the gesture had ended up being the gateway to lifting that burden off her chest.

Wyatt wouldn't lie to himself. He loved women, maybe a little too much, and they loved him back. He had taken what they gave and given what he could. He had left a lot of broken hearts in his wake, and always believed it wasn't his fault. Most of the women knew what they were getting into. A little fun and that was it. Problems only arose when they got what was mutually agreed and then, they wanting to change him to make him theirs alone. That's when he usually vanished.

Four days had passed since the night of December eighth.

His passion for Claudia was clearly out of this world. She had given herself to him, and since that night, he had been rethinking his views about women. This was the one he wouldn't let get away.

He couldn't get enough of her. It wasn't the sex. They'd done it every way possible, and he hadn't gotten enough. There was a void in him, and she'd filled it. Now he lived in fear of losing her. He was acting like some of the women he'd dated, very insecure.

For a change, Wyatt was on the receiving end of matters of the heart. His greatest threat was Max Steel. He usually wouldn't have cared, but he'd seen the way the guy went all soft and lovey-dovey when Claudia was around.

Wyatt didn't give a crap about him, but he cared about how Claudia responded to him. As if she had a perpetual crush on the guy.

For the first time in his life, Wyatt understood the heartache felt by the women he used and then discarded. He'd never had an inkling that could happen to him. But the thought that it could was real. She'd given herself to him, but he still found himself wanting more. It wasn't just sex. It was much more.

Claudia was in his head all the time. A part of him thought all he had to do was shut his eyes and they'd be together. Hell, he didn't even need to close his eyes to see her face in his mind's eye. See every contour of her face, her smile, feel the smoothness of her skin and what it smelled like when he kissed her hand, a clean, fresh, flowery smell.

"Are you even listening to me?" asked Max.

Wyatt was brought back to the present. "Sorry, can you say it again?"

Max repeated himself. They were understaffed, and two customers were coming in tonight. Anything that would keep

Claudia's load light and keep Max away from her would be good.

"So what do you think is the best way to handle it?"

"You already have an established team that takes you to the north side of the resort. It doesn't make sense to have you going back and forth. I'll absorb the newcomers into my group, and Claudia's load will remain unchanged."

Max seemed to think for a moment, then nodded. "Okay, that should work."

They'd reached an amicable plan both were happy with, until that evening when the couple arrived, and it was déjà vu all over again. Women throwing themselves at him, and their men feeling very insecure.

That night, exhausted, he retired for the night with Claudia. He hoped the next day, with the beginning of coaching, would keep the Riley girl occupied and her mind focused on something else.

It worked. Riley was occupied, all right. But she tasked herself with making sure her instructor never left her sight.

Wyatt had been skiing and skating all day. Riley had gotten on him like dust on a piece of sticky tape. He'd obliged her, hoping that attending to her would satisfy her curiosity about him.

But so far, her fascination was still very much alive.

Wyatt's heart almost broke when he had to send Claudia off on her own. He wished he had shut down the training and left with her when she'd called him. She hadn't looked happy when she walked away. Wyatt hoped she knew it was all for the best.

Then there was the issue of Cameron Dawn. They had history all right, and the way things were going right now, they might as well be back in college.

13

Claudia

CLAUDIA WALKED TOWARD THE FIREPLACE WHERE MAX SAT. The closer she got to him, the more she wondered what she was going to say. The number one thing driving her was curiosity, and the second, boredom. Wyatt was not here.

For the past few days, it had been just the two of them together, then tonight, he'd decided to spend their quality time with Riley.

Thinking about Riley should propel her forward. But she was also held back by possible blowback. Nicole and Max had been friends. Nicole might not be happy with her for talking to him. *Don't be silly*, she told herself. Nicole had known Max ages ago, and now she was happily married. Still, Claudia dragged her feet. The fireplace was just a few feet from the window, but somehow the distance had stretched in her mind.

In the background, Jim Reeve's version of Jingle Bells wafted from the speakers and mixed with the sound of conversations. The clinking and clanking of cutlery on plates made it seem like she was back in Hawks Lair.

The mention of 'sleigh' in the song reminded Claudia of what had happened on the sleigh ride with Max. Was it intentional? Was it an accident? Either way, it had left her wondering what an unequivocal touch from him would feel like.

The closer Claudia got to Max, the more she felt the warmth radiating from the fireplace on her skin, warm and comforting. The crackling sound made by the burning wood as fire licked it reminded her of another safe and comfortable time before her childhood had been shattered.

It reminded her of her father in their living room when she was small, sitting in his La-Z-Boy by the fire, reading, or watching TV.

Claudia enjoyed sitting on his lap. He would read her a story from one of the fairy tale books they had in the house. Her favorite was Little Red Riding Hood. She could relate to that story. There were woods around them, and she used to explore them like Little Red.

Sometimes Daddy would make up his own stories and tell them as she rested on his chest. Eventually, she would doze off, cocooned in the safest place of all, her father's arms, with the beating of his heart as a lullaby.

All that came to a staggering halt after the accident. Claudia lost her mother, her sisters, her father, and herself. Even though nobody came right out and blamed her, it was her actions that had led to their mother being where she was. Her relationship with her father was never the same. She was all alone.

Max Steel was too young to be her father. But back then, he'd hung out with Nicole, and as a young man, he'd shown so much confidence in himself, and perhaps that was what had attracted her to him.

Claudia was now a few feet away from Max, her heart hammering in her chest. He waved his mug of something to the beat of the music. Then he turned and saw her.

Max's eyes widened. He sprang to his feet. "Claudia! Everything okay?" He looked around the room. "Did anything happen?"

Claudia gripped her mug tighter. Now she was apprehensive. "No, everything is fine. I just saw you and decided to come over."

Max's eyes dashed around again. "You just saw me? You see me every day. Are you sure there's no problem?"

Claudia was scared. She'd heard about people that came back from wars losing it. She met his gaze. "Yes, I'm sure. I just came over to say hello. So hello."

Max's eyes stopped dashing around and focused on her. His chest rose as he sucked in air, and fell when he let it out, his eyes never leaving hers.

Claudia turned to walk away.

He raised both palms. "Oh, I'm really sorry." He pointed at the sofa opposite him. "Please join me."

"Are you sure? I only came to-"

"I'd be honored," said Max, cutting her off. "What are you drinking? Can I get you another one?"

Claudia sat down, looked at his eyes, and then at her mug. He had the most beautiful eyes. "It's just coffee, with some whiskey."

Max laughed. "One of those Paul's specials? It goes with the weather. I'm having one myself." He raised his mug.

"Paul is the bartender?"

"Yes."

"Anyway, let me get you more."

"No. I think I'm fine."

"I need some myself. Give me a minute, I'll be right back."

Claudia watched him go. He was probably over six feet tall with broad shoulders. She liked his quiet confidence and wondered what his story was. What had happened that made him a loner? Probably something that had to do with the military. Claudia pondered if she should ask him about the sleigh ride. *Hey Max, I have a question. That day on the slopes, did you mean to squeeze my thighs and grab my crotch?* It didn't even sound good in her mind. Imagine saying such a thing out loud. Just then, Max turned around from the bar and started to come back with two mugs.

"Here you go," he said and placed the mugs on the table.

"I didn't want one."

"Please indulge me. Its only coffee." He winked.

"Okay." Claudia reached for hers. "Thanks." She took a sip. "Hmm, sweet."

"Yes, I asked him to make it the way I like it. Espresso, Irish cream, and some sugar." Max took a sip and let out a satisfied sigh.

"So do you like it here?"

"Well, I come back every year. probably more like, I'm used to it now." Claudia tilted her head. "I don't hate it."

"Same with me. Something to do during the winter months and play around in the snow. How's Nicole? I heard she got married."

Claudia smiled. "She's fine. She got married to Eben."

"Somebody we know?"

"Well, now we know him. The family bought the Eastman estate, and Nicole and Eben met, and it worked for them." Claudia felt all warm and fuzzy inside. Max was so easy to talk to. Why hadn't she done this all along?

"Ah." Max sighed and rubbed his hands on his jeans. "The one that got away."

"I don't think that's the way it happened."

Max leaned forward, his lips curled in feigned dismay. "What? People are discussing me?"

"No, that's not how it happened. It was all your fault. Even though I was little, I remember. Then you were a young man eager-"

"Were a young man? I'm still young. I'm just thirty-two."

"Compared to my twenty-two, you're ancient," Claudia laughed. "Okay, when you were a lot younger, you couldn't wait to get out of Mountain Peak, and the army was your ticket out. As soon as you were old enough, you ran off."

"You were monitoring me?"

"Maybe."

Max fell back into his chair. He shook his head, then sat up again. "I just wanted to see the world. I was afraid time was passing me by."

"Ironic. Now you're back in Mountain Peak. You went full circle."

Max chuckled. "I saw more than I bargained for and ran back."

Claudia hadn't known he would be so easy to talk to. She wanted to say that. She opened her mouth, then closed it.

"You wanted to say something."

"Well, I never knew you'd be so easy to talk to. You always look so serious, like an angry dad."

"What? Like an angry dad?" Max shook his head. "I didn't know that. I'm just a boring person, and I don't want people talking to me and finding out, so I keep a stern face."

"I don't think you're boring. Maybe it's more of finding someone who shares the same things as you."

Max laughed. "Exactly. There's nothing to share. The

only stories I have are war stories, and it's not something I enjoy reliving."

"I'm sure you're interesting. Where are you going once you leave here?"

"Easy. Home!"

Claudia leaned forward. She felt a little buzzed. "You're not going to stop anywhere?"

"No, straight home. Maybe stop for a second to enjoy a view, and that's it." Max shrugged. "I can show you. It's nothing impressive."

Claudia thought that was boring, but she was determined to prove he was not. "Okay, show me." She drained the rest of her coffee.

Max threw on his coat, and she did the same.

14

Claudia

CLAUDIA FOLLOWED MAX OUTSIDE TO THE BACK OF THE lounge building. With the sun gone and just stepping out from a warm room, the cold stung her face like little needles. A faint smell of fried food from the lounge's kitchen exhaust hung in the air.

The wind howled.

Mix that with the dull *boom boom boom* coming from the lounge, it created what Claudia imagined the Dementors in Harry Potter would sound like.

Claudia glanced at the skating rink where Wyatt had been instructing Ms. Cutie. It was now empty.

The wind tore the breath out of her reach. She'd grown up here and was used to this weather. She lowered her head to inhale and zipped her jacket all the way up.

They went beyond a cluster of pine trees behind the lounge, which Claudia now realized was placed there as a windbreaker to protect the buildings.

Max looked at her, extended his right arm out as if presenting an award, and smiled. "Voila."

A frozen winter landscape was laid out in front of them, including the tall peak that the town had gotten its name from.

"It's nice," said Claudia. She'd seen it before. So much so that it didn't take her breath away anymore.

"Yes, but wait. There's more."

Maybe it was the alcohol, but Max being close to her with a big smile on his face made her feel...gosh, she couldn't find the word for it. She felt good inside.

As it got darker, the wind twirled a cloud of loose snow in the air. Against that backdrop, the moon seemed to soar into the night sky and rise above the mountain peaks. Its light glistened off the snow capturing a picturesque frozen wonderland that would make for a beautiful screen saver.

"Wow, it's beautiful."

Laughter bubbled out of Max. "Oh yeah?"

"Yes!" Claudia reached into her pocket, brought out her phone, and took a couple of pictures.

Max nodded. "It gets me too, each time I'm out here. You should see the sunset or sunrise in the desert. Also amazing."

Claudia looked at him. "Really? I'd love to see that."

"So we have something in common, we both appreciate nature. I would never have guessed."

"Max, this is not boring at all!" The light glistening off the snow made it look like twilight. Claudia's eyes were fixed on his face. As she watched, the smile faded from his face. It turned gloomy and shut. Claudia's pulse quickened. She looked around but saw nothing. "What...What is it?"

"We have to go." Max's face returned to its everyday demeanor, his eyebrows almost knitted together. "Sorry I brought you here." He turned and started walking away fast toward the lounge.

Claudia trudged through the snow as fast as she could to keep up. She thought they'd made a connection there. And without warning, it had broken apart. "What did I do?"

Max didn't answer her and didn't say a word again until they got to the parking lot of the lounge.

"Have a good night, Claudia." He walked toward the parking lot. The headlamps of a Ford F-150 flashed as he approached. Max opened the door and got in. Moments later, the engine roared into life, and he drove away.

15

Max

IN HIS REARVIEW MIRROR, MAX COULD SEE CLAUDIA standing there, watching his car drive away. She looked like a toddler watching a parent go off to work even though they'd rather have them stay at home. He watched as she walked away, shoulders slumped, past the lounge and toward the accommodation entrance.

Max felt a painful lump in his throat, and when he swallowed, it wouldn't go away. Why was he always behaving like an idiot? He felt a tug in his heart. Like someone had died, and there was just nothing he could do about it.

He drove past Main Street, and Christmas was in the air. The streets were alive with people hurrying back and forth. He stopped at the light. Close to the mall hotel stood a Salvation Army Santa, tolling his bell with a big smile on his face.

The traffic light changed, and traffic started to move again. Max headed toward the hills where very few people lived. As he passed the last traffic light before leaving Main Street, he saw yet another Santa. This one had a kettle that said, Marshal Novelty Store. Everyone now had a Santa, he thought.

But what struck him was that this Santa and the last one he saw were both smiling and looked happy. Truth be told, what was there to be happy about standing in the cold, ringing a bell all night, harassing people to give you a donation, and being ignored most of the time?

But every Christmas, they showed up again and again. They were happy, and they did what made them happy.

Max knew it was the exception to the rule to see anyone that had gone through life without some adversity.

He smiled as he remembered a public speaker he'd seen on YouTube say that problems and challenges are a part of life. Either we're neck-deep in one already, we've just gotten out of a jam, or a new problem was just about to make itself known. It was a constant.

In other words, problems were always there. Nobody would come and steal your problem. Max laughed out loud at that thought. You can't sweep it under the carpet. It's out of sight, but guess what, once you lift the rug, it's right there. You must learn to deal with it and continue living.

Max gunned the F-150 up the hill, leaving behind him the downtown of Mountain Peak. He wished he had left the problems that lived in his mind on the battlefield of Afghanistan where they happened. Love could be taken away from you at the snap of a finger. He had firsthand knowledge, but he must continue living.

Claudia had always been there, his soul mate, waiting for him, but he hadn't realized it. He'd better clean up his act and stop acting weird around her before he lost her forever, especially now that there was competition.

Wyatt Webb. Maybe he should lure him into a web and disappear him.

Max wound down the windows and took a deep breath. It cleared his head and removed any murderous thoughts from his mind. Uphill, the air was cleaner and smelled fresh. He was closer to his log cabin where his neighbors were the bears, foxes, and deer that wandered over every now and then.

Max's heart felt lighter. He had a plan. Tomorrow, he would find Claudia. And start fixing things.

16

Claudia

STILL TRYING TO PROCESS THE ABRUPT CHANGE IN MAX, Claudia walked into the lobby of the lodge. She welcomed the warmth and was glad the hallway was empty. She was in no mood to talk to anybody. Again, she found herself close to Jane's door, her old room, and turned around.

She contemplated going to Wyatt's room but didn't want to find Riley in his bed, considering how she was flirting with him. Claudia liked Wyatt, but they were not officially dating. Still, if she found Riley in his room, that would be too much for one night, considering Max's behavior toward her.

Claudia ran the evening events through her mind, trying to figure out if she'd done anything that triggered Max's response. She came up empty. Claudia consoled herself that this behavior wasn't so different from his past behavior. He'd always kept to himself. And this evening was the first time he'd ever opened up. Well, she wasn't going to burden herself with thoughts of whether she'd offended him or not. She didn't want to swap the guilt she felt over her mother's death with that of offending Max.

Claudia unlocked her door, stepped in, and turned on the light. She froze. Wyatt was sprawled on her bed, fast asleep. He was fully clothed, and Claudia knew he was just completely exhausted from coaching Riley.

Claudia smiled; Riley had lost out. She went to the bathroom, brushed her teeth, washed her face, and changed into her nightgown. Soon she too was fast asleep.

Claudia dreamed of Max. She was chasing him, trying to find out why he'd ended their discussion so abruptly. Each time she got close to catching him, he would get away.

Soon Claudia felt a hand on her shoulder rocking her. When she opened her eyes, it was Wyatt all dressed. "Hey."

Wyatt smiled. "Good morning. Sorry about yesterday. By the time we finally called it a night, I was so tired. I'd planned to stay up and wait for you, but sleep claimed me." He rubbed the back of his hand on her chin. "Did you sleep well?"

Claudia stretched and nodded.

"It's time to go do it all again."

"I wish we could just sleep in."

Wyatt leaned forward and kissed her on the cheek. "Same here. That Riley's something else. I was hoping she would get exhausted, but she just kept on wanting more." He shook his head. "I hope today will be easier. My plan is to give her all the instructions she feels she needs, and then move on."

"That might work," said Claudia. "I remember Ron saying she really wanted to learn so badly. You have an overzealous student on your hands."

"She's a model," said Wyatt. "She doesn't need to be an expert, just pose and look like she knows what she's doing."

Claudia felt a prick in her heart when Wyatt said *model*.

How was she going to compete? Wanting to get up, she pulled the blanket aside. Her nightgown had ridden up, exposing her panties. She saw Wyatt's eyes flicker and focus on her waist.

"Don't tell me you have the energy for that," Claudia teased. She pulled down her nightgown. "I don't want you to have an accident on the slopes. Too tired to steer your ski away from a tree."

"I'll always have the energy for you, but you have a point. Let's leave it for later in the evening."

"Does Riley know you have other students to coach?"

"Yes, I told her. And she said she was one of them."

Claudia rolled her eyes. "Is she like a high maintenance model?"

Wyatt got up and sighed. "I don't know, but hopefully, she'll be too tired herself and won't show up today." He kissed her on the lips. "I have to go."

"I better get up too. See you this evening?" Claudia raised an eyebrow.

"You bet."

As soon as Wyatt left, Claudia went to the bathroom, took a shower, and got dressed in her usual outdoor gear. She grabbed her phone and noticed she had a text from Max. Her pulse started to race. About time he apologized. She wondered if she should tell Wyatt about him. Not that anything was going on, just in the same way he told her about Riley and her antics. Maybe when she saw him tonight.

Claudia tapped the screen and perused the text as she headed for the lodge exit. She stopped in her tracks. It wasn't what she'd expected at all. It was about work. A fucking work email, instead of an apology.

Max wanted her to report to the pond closer to the woods

and the cable car terminal, where skiers would board the lift to the slopes.

Disappointed, Claudia sighed, then sent a reply that she would be there. She put her phone in her pocket and continued toward the exit, wondering if she should get coffee from the coffee machine in the lounge. Opening that pond also meant that more people had signed up to skate and ski. Christmas was in the air. She opted to get coffee.

At this time of the morning, the lounge was a far cry from last night. Nobody was there.

Most ski resort customers drive up for a few hours of skiing or skating, then go back to their homes or hotels in Mountain Peak or in neighboring towns.

The smell of coffee greeted her once she entered the room. Claudia helped herself. She decided to drink it black.

"Hi Claudia. Good morning," said a voice behind her.

Claudia looked over her shoulder. It was Ron. She smiled. "Hi!" She snapped on the lid to the takeaway cup. "How are you?" her eyes dashed around. No Riley. "You're an early bird too?" There was a calmness about Ron that she liked. He focused on the person he was talking to. He was like the boy next door. Or the boy at school that crushed on you and carried your books. Because that was the only way he knew at that level to express he liked you.

"It depends. Riley is already up, and I thought I'd get some shots of her this morning, and get feedback about the photos I emailed her. But I think they went up with the cable car already."

"Oh," said Claudia. "You can grab the next car and head out there too."

"Yes, I know. Just came to get coffee while I waited. The operator said I had to wait for the same cable car to come back."

"Okay, that makes sense." Claudia stepped aside to let him grab a cup of coffee. "I'm headed in that direction too. There's a pond out there we want to get ready for skating. As Christmas approaches, we get more customers, so some of the traffic would be directed there."

"Nice," said Ron and nodded. "I'll walk with you then if you don't mind."

"Of course not. Let's go." Claudia was surprised to learn that Ron and Wyatt had been at NYU at the same time. She wanted to ask him if they knew each other, but just then, Max drove by on a snowmobile.

"Hi Cameron!" said Max over the rumble of the vehicle.

Ron waved.

"Hop on, Claudia! We have to sweep snow off the surface of the pond to get it ready for guests. I got an email from the manager that a bunch of people will be coming our way today."

Claudia was taken aback. Granted, this was a job, there was no telltale sign of remorse about last night on Max's face. She was not a switch to be turned off and on as the need arose. Why should she get on the vehicle?

Max waited and seconds ticked by. It started to look awkward. She leaned closer to Ron, smiled, and said, "See you later. Have fun on the slopes." She pointed at the approaching lift. "Your ride is coming too."

Ron looked at where she pointed. "About time. You take care too."

Claudia got on behind Max, and for a second, was flustered on what to do with her cup.

Max reached for her cup. "Give me that." He snatched it from Claudia and snapped it into the coffee holder on the steering column.

"Easy, dude. I'm not one of your army buddies."

Max chuckled. "Hold on tight."

The machine took off.

They stopped at the pond. Two workers were already there, removing shrubs and clearing dead leaves and dried tree branches from the ponds. Max smiled at her and showed her how to use a push brush to remove the remaining snow on the surface to reveal the ice. He was now back to smiling and happy, thought Claudia.

"You can test it out if you want," said Max, smiling. "I know I will."

Claudia sighed. What a complicated man. Mean and hard one moment and smiling the next. "I didn't bring any skates."

"You wear size nine, right? I brought you some."

Claudia tried not to show the surprise on her face. Maybe that was his way of saying he was sorry.

Max gave her a patronizing tone. "Please join me?"

That tone, and the fact he knew her size did it for Claudia. It was like he acknowledged he'd messed up, and that was as far as his over-sized ego would let him go. "Okay."

"I'll race you," said Max once they had their skates on.

Claudia went after him and soon they were skating around the pond. The trees made the scenery look like a pond in a park. But most of all, Max was all smiles. She'd never seen him that happy.

"I'll let them know the pond is ready," said Max and pulled out his cell phone. "So they can start sending the guests over." He skated to the edge of the pond and raised the phone to his ears.

While he was on the phone, Claudia skated around, executing some routines she thought she'd forgotten from her competitive skating days. Jumps, spins; you name it. She was rusty and heavier now, but soon, she executed those moves in what appeared to be a flawless performance. Feeling dizzy, she did a final spin, stopped, and bowed. Claudia heard clapping and turned.

"Wow. I didn't know you were that good," said Max. "You're full of surprises."

And so are you. But Claudia didn't say it out loud. "Thank you."

"Hey, listen, I'm going up to the mountains tomorrow morning to visit an old mountain man friend of mine. Since we like the same things, I think you'd enjoy it. Will you come with me?"

Claudia remembered telling Wyatt they would meet up tonight. "I don't know." She might be too tired tomorrow. But she didn't want to turn Max down either.

"You have other engagements?"

"Kind of." Claudia saw a flash of disappointment flash across his face, but he regrouped quickly.

Max clapped his gloved hands together. "Let's do this then. You know the place of mist? There's a-"

"Place of mist!"

"Place of mist!" said Max, mimicking Claudia. "Keep your clothes on. We're not going to run around naked in the thermal pool. In fact, we're not even going there. Opposite the place of mist is Fox Run Ridge. That's where we're going."

Claudia nodded. She'd heard of it but never hiked it herself.

"Good. I'll be there until 8 am tomorrow morning. If you're not there by then, I'll go ahead, okay? It's a scenic walk to the old man's cabin."

Claudia nodded. "Okay, fair enough."

17

CAMERON

THE CABLE CAR MOVED WITH A JERK, AND RON GRABBED A horizontal bar on the side to steady himself. It reminded him of one of the many days he'd taken the subway to the office and had to stand.

The cable was packed like a subway car in New York City during rush hour, but at least most of the people were smiling. Some looked anxious, like Ron. Probably they didn't like heights and maybe were not too enthused about all this running around in the snow, but needed to be there for one reason or another.

Gradually the cable car climbed higher and higher, and in Ron's eyes transformed from a subway car to an airplane within minutes. Both were his least favorite means of transportation. His stomach tightened, and he tried to think of good things. The scenery was lovely. The glass window gave him a nice view of the snow-covered landscape, but the height wasn't helping. All Ron could think of was, what if the cable cut?

He thought of Riley Carter, and his mood soured. He'd been covering her for some time now and had fallen in love with her. They had a platonic relationship, which he hoped would gradually translate into a relationship.

Since they arrived, if she wasn't on the phone with her agent, Mary, she was with Wyatt. Ron had high hopes that the god of love by proximity would smile his way.

It worked for Britney Spears and Kevin Federline. Kevin was her dancer. Ethan Hawke married Ryan Shawhughes, his kids' nanny, in 2010. One thing leading to another. You know how these things go. Rob Lowe married Sheryl Berkoff, his makeup artist, in 2011. Well, maybe next would be 'Supermodel Riley Carter Marries Her Photographer, Cameron Dawn.'

A gust of wind tossed the cable car around, bringing him back to reality. "Jesus," he muttered, his balls tightening. People perished in plane crashes all the time. He would die just a few feet from the ground in a cable car crash—such shitty luck.

Ron looked outside the window and noticed they were approaching their terminal. Thank God. Not too far from where they would stop, he also saw the unmistakable figure in white, his beloved Riley, now throwing herself at Wyatt. Maybe it was nothing. Riley was always too friendly, too *handsy*. He knew she'd always talked about learning how to ski and skate, but the way she was running around Wyatt made her look like a dog in heat.

His mind drifted to Claudia. She was a breath of fresh air. Friendly, down to earth, and very pretty too. Why were all the good girls always taken? He couldn't even understand why Wyatt, of all people, was the lucky guy, the guy she'd fallen for. And then Riley dropped into his lap. He knew Webb - the man without scruples. Ron was sure if it had been summer, and Riley was in a skirt trying to rollerblade, Wyatt would have slid in a long time ago.

Looking out of the window, he saw Wyatt fawning over Riley. That dog. He hadn't changed his ways. At a point, they'd have to acknowledge they knew each other unless this photoshoot ended sooner rather than later. He thought of Riley falling for Wyatt's antics, and heat flashed through his body, his heartbeat pounding in his ears. History repeating itself—that would be the last straw. This time, he wasn't going to turn the other cheek or take it lying down.

Suddenly the tune to Rod Stewart's *Some Guys Have All the Luck* started to play.

"You must be kidding me," muttered Ron under his breath. He looked around.

"Hello! Mommy?" said a female voice.

Ron shook his head. It was somebody's ring tone. If it wasn't for bad luck, he wouldn't have any luck at all.

18

Claudia

CLAUDIA LEFT MAX AND HEADED BACK TO TAKE CARE OF HER students for the day. She was teaching a bunch of kids the basics of snowboarding. Max said another instructor would coach the kids until she got there.

Luckily, the pond thing didn't take that long, and from the look of it, Max just wanted to invite her for a date.

Claudia stopped walking as the implication hit her.

"Oh my God," she said in a whisper. After all these years, he was asking her on a date.

When Claudia started to walk again, there was a spring in her step. She smiled and waved at people she passed on the way as if they were her long-lost friends. She got to her group and joined the person Max had assigned to her.

Claudia noticed one of the kids didn't have her boot secured and walked her through the right way to do it.

"Safety first!" one of the kids said.

"Safety first," others chorused.

Claudia had the kids sit on the snow, and she and the other instructor helped them buckle their boots to the snowboard. It was always fun working with kids when it was their first time snowboarding.

Claudia did three classes, and soon it was time to call it a day. The parents always lurked around as the kids were taught. They materialized once the class was over. She released the last set to their parents.

When she was done, Claudia walked back to the rink closest to the lounge. She'd spent a better part of the morning with three different groups of kids, and the instructions always the same. They started with safety and ended with the kids snowboarding, some with support, and some without. It was afternoon when she headed to the lounge, confident that Wyatt would be there since he'd had an early start.

To her surprise, Wyatt was still skating with Riley. Claudia shook her head in disbelief. "But the girl's got stamina though," said Claudia in a low voice. She watched them for a few minutes, and Riley's skills had indeed improved. Definitely better than yesterday. She was an intense student.

Claudia turned to the *click click click* of a camera shutter.

Dressed as an Eskimo and looking cool and calculated, Ron was in character taking pictures. She watched him adjust the camera lens, followed by the repeated high-speed shutter sound. Claudia enjoyed watching photographers at work. She always wondered what exactly made them decide *Yes, this is the time to push the button.*

Her eyes were on him when his face kind of went sour, and a vein on his temple throbbed. He took his eyes away from the camera, hissed, and turned away.

Claudia looked at Riley and Wyatt, and she too shook her head. Riley had fallen yet again, and she and Wyatt were on the ground. Claudia felt sorry for Ron, now understanding his discomfort.

It didn't look like he and Riley were a couple, more like he loved her from afar.

Claudia couldn't watch anymore. She could get a drink in the lounge or go back to her room and wait for Wyatt. She paused for a moment and wondered why suddenly her life seemed to revolve around him.

She realized she'd been punching her right fist into her left palm as the eighth of December popped into her mind. Wyatt had lifted a burden from her mind, and things had been going great for them until Riley arrived.

Claudia reminded herself that she didn't have any claim on Wyatt. She hoped that maybe after Wyatt gave Riley all the training she felt she needed, she would stop hovering around him.

Claudia looked at Ron, who now had his back to the rink, and felt sorry for him. It was time she was out of here herself. Claudia didn't want to be as dejected as he was. She opted to go to the lounge.

Once Claudia stepped in, the warmth of the lounge enveloped her, reminding her you couldn't just stay outdoors in the winter without being active.

Paul, the barman, was there. Since Max had told her his name after seeing him there forever, it somehow changed how she felt about him. He was no longer just a bartender. Claudia now felt obliged to at least discuss the weather with him.

"Hello, Paul. I have to apologize that I never asked you your name before."

Paul froze. "Who told you my name was Paul?"

Claudia's eyes widened. Was she getting Max into trouble? Her default was to always tell the truth if she wasn't sure which way the answer would go. "Ummm…Max."

Paul pointed to a corner where a couple of cardboard boxes lay on the floor. "That Max?"

Max was hunched over one of the boxes. He seemed to be rummaging for something.

Claudia's heart hammered in her chest. "No," she said slowly. Her nostrils flared. She wasn't a good liar. Paul would see through her. Or whoever he was.

Paul stared at her for what seemed like a long moment, with no emotion whatsoever. Then he smiled. "Okay, you can call me Paul."

Claudia exhaled, only realizing she had stopped breathing when he stared at her.

"Oh my God, you should have seen your face," said Paul. "I didn't mean to alarm you. Max and I were in the army together before. I was his CO before I retired. You like him, eh?"

Claudia was sure her color had changed like a chameleon, especially since she'd just come in from outside. She didn't know what to answer, so she avoided that question and asked her own. "What's a CO?"

Paul threw his head back and laughed some more.

Claudia watched him. He looked like he was in his late thirties. By the time he stopped laughing, tears had streamed down his cheeks.

"I'm so sorry. Please forgive me. You're so…just, never go into a profession where you'll have to lie for a living." He wiped his eyes. "So what can I get you?"

Claudia wanted to say coffee, then stopped. "Hold on. I'll be back." She walked over to Max. "Hi."

Max looked up, and a huge smile stretched his lips when he saw it was her. "Hey, are you done for the day?"

"Kind of. What're you doing?"

"Oh, some of the guys wanted to have a before Christmas dance tonight. I'm trying to turn the lounge into a dance floor." He opened the box to show some lights and a disco ball.

"Really?" said Claudia. No one had told her.

"I found some lights in storage. I won't be here anyway. I'm just going to leave it out for them to set up as they like." Max closed the flap of the boxes and pushed them against the wall. "I have to run some errands for tomorrow. Get some supplies for the Fox Run trip." Max stacked one box on another. "I hope you can make it."

Claudia gave a non-committal smile.

"I have to go." Max squeezed her shoulder as he passed.

A lot was happening so fast. Claudia turned around and watched Max as he exited the lounge. She walked back to her stool. "Hey, Paul, can I have that special coffee of yours now, please?"

"Sure, give me a minute."

Minutes later, Paul brought Claudia her coffee. She took a sip, and it hit the right spot. It calmed her down. She nursed the drink, wondering what to do. She'd just taken the last sip when Wyatt walked in with Riley. Ron brought up the rear, unzipping his Eskimo suit as he walked.

Wyatt waved at Claudia and headed her way, while Riley continued to one of the sofas.

"Hey, I thought you'd be out there by the rink?" said Wyatt.

"I was. You didn't see me?"

Wyatt ran his hand along the back of his neck. "I don't doubt you." He leaned closer to Claudia. "I've been trying to get her off my back."

"Well, it seems like you've finally succeeded."

Wyatt groaned. "I wish." He shook his head. "There's this dance I just heard about for tonight."

"Yeah, I saw Max bringing out the paraphernalia," said Claudia and pointed to the boxes in the corner. "What do you mean, you wish? Are you now her chaperon?"

A burst of laughter escaped Wyatt's lips. He shook his head, removed his hat, and combed his hair with his fingers.

Claudia's stomach churned. "Who are you taking to the dance?"

19

WYATT

THE ANSWER TO WHO WYATT WAS TAKING TO THE DANCE wasn't as easy as it seemed. How do you punch someone in the face and make them understand and agree with you that you had to do it?

Wyatt exhaled. The lounge's sounds reminded him of the times as a kid when he placed a bowel over his head and spoke. All the sounds had coalesced into one loud distant echo.

His eyes dashed around the lounge, looking for something to save him from providing an answer.

He ran his fingers through his hair again. At the pace his mind raced, it could easily break the fastest downhill skiing record. He looked into Claudia's eyes and immediately glanced away. They were like lasers that seemed to pierce his chest, reach into his rib cage, and squeeze his heart. He'd let her down.

"Wyatt?"

Her voice was shaky as she said his name. His silence was already hurting her. Wyatt could see that in her eyes. Her nostrils flared, and her lips twitched. He couldn't lie to her.

"Oh, mmm..." He stroked his jaw. "Riley brought it up. I don't even know how she heard about the dance. Now I'm beginning to think it was she that planted the seed of the idea...I'll be going with her."

Her face tight, Claudia exhaled, her lips a thin line. "You didn't even think of asking me first?"

Wyatt saw his opening and took it. "I'm just seeing you for the first time since I heard about it. I should have said no to her, but you know how she is." Wyatt's voice faded as the last words left his lips.

Claudia's eyes were on him. She moved her lips as if she wanted to say something, then bit her lower lip.

Wyatt's mind started to relax. Claudia seemed to be taking it well. Something in her was invigorating. He should have stopped there, but he decided to continue. "Claudia, honestly, I didn't know you would be interested. In fact, I didn't think you owned any evening dresses." As soon as the words came out, Wyatt knew it hadn't come out right. He raised his palms in an *I surrender* gesture and tried to get his foot out of his mouth. "I didn't mean that literally, of course."

"What time is the dance?"

The look on her face made Wyatt feel like he'd kicked a puppy. He looked at his watch as most people do when the question is about time, even though the answer wasn't there. Any distraction from looking at her face was welcome.

"Seven."

Claudia got off the stool, gave Wyatt one of those lips only smiles, and walked away.

"Claudia!" He went after her.

She raised her palm up without looking back as if saying *Don't worry about me.*

He looked at her, struggling with himself not to go after her. To obey her wishes.

"Wyatt," said a female voice.

He turned to the voice. It was Riley. She smiled and waved at him to come over. He turned and gave Claudia a fleeting look before she disappeared through the door. "Women," he muttered to himself and headed toward Riley.

20

Claudia

CLAUDIA WALKED AS FAST AS SHE COULD AWAY FROM WYATT. She hoped he had taken the cue from her raised hand and not come after her. She didn't want to deal with him apologizing for not asking her to the dance.

It was what Wyatt wanted.

No, it was what *Riley* wanted.

There was no beating about the bush on this one. There are blondes, and there are *blondes*. Riley was a knockout, with supermodel potential. Claudia herself wasn't interested in women, and didn't know Riley's preferences, but if Riley Carter somehow found her way into her bed while she was snoozing, she would feign sleep and let her put her *Roman hands* and *Russian* fingers to work.

This time Claudia found her room without going to the old one first. If they wanted each other, they could have each other.

She entered her room and sat on her bed. Claudia held her

head in her hands and took a deep breath. She wouldn't...
shouldn't let this get to her.

If Claudia looked at it constructively, Wyatt was right.
She was not that graceful on heels and didn't have a lot of
dresses. As a kid growing up, especially after Mother's death,
she was mostly left to her own devices. She would go for
long walks on her own, exploring the woods, fishing with
boys she met in the forest, and doing what boys love to do.
Being the last person to be selected in a game because boys
are chosen first. Come nightfall, the boys would hang out in
the mall with other girls, not bothering about Claudia because
they considered her one of them.

It had never bothered her until right this moment. Claudia
knew she wasn't that pretty but at least could get heads to
turn. No, she wouldn't let this define her.

She sprang to her feet and opened her suitcase. At the
bottom was a dress and a black thong that had always been
there. The red dress with black trim and the thong had both
been gifts from her Aunt Sam. She'd worn the dress once,
had it dry cleaned, and left it at the bottom of her traveling
suitcase for emergencies like tonight. The thong she hadn't
bothered with. She preferred lacy boy-shorts.

Claudia brought it out and ironed it. But the lines and
wrinkles on it for having lived at the bottom of the suitcase
for God knows how long wouldn't go away. Her newly
minted hope faded right in front of her.

She tipped her head backward to face the ceiling and
exhaled. Then she let it flop forward. Shoulders slumped, she
let out a deep sigh. Should she fight it or let it go? You
couldn't force a man that didn't want you to like you. That
was stalking.

But he did want her.

It was just that Riley was distracting him.

Claudia decided to take a hot shower. Maybe she would feel better after that; at least get a good night's sleep for her trouble.

Claudia took her clothes off and headed for the bathroom. An idea she'd read in some magazine popped into her head. She went to the bathroom and turned on the water to the hottest. Then she grabbed a hanger from the closet and hung her dress on it. When she returned to the bathroom, the air was thick with steam.

She hung the dress on the curtain railing on the outside of the shower curtain, away from the water. She reduced the hot water to what she could tolerate. It still produced steam. Then she took a long shower. When she was done twenty minutes later and examined the dress, all the wrinkles were gone.

It was 7:30 pm when Claudia left her room. She was dressed in the red dress and stilettos, looking like she was ready for a photoshoot.

The *boom boom boom* of music as she approached the lounge from the lodge area resonated inside her. She stood outside the closed lounge door, and for a second wasn't sure if coming back was the right thing to do. Pulse racing, she took a deep breath, opened the door, and walked in.

The heat from more than a few bodies in an enclosed area and the smell of sweat and different perfumes hit her once she stepped in. The Claudia who walked into the lounge was different to the one who had left earlier. This one was on the offensive.

The music was now distinct, a track from an up and coming new artist. Men and women danced in the middle of the room where couches and sofas had been moved to create a dance floor. Their gyrating bodies were captured as still images each time a strobe light fell on them.

Claudia stood close to the door and glanced around,

looking for Wyatt. Reflected light from the disco ball in the ceiling bounced off people as she searched. It always amazed her how fast a dance floor filled up once the word *party* was thrown around.

Some couples left the dance floor, and some remained as the music faded out, and another one started. That was when Claudia spotted Wyatt. He was dressed in a dark blazer and button-down shirt. He stood at the edge of the dance floor, watching people.

Wyatt looked around, glanced at the door, and looked away. Then he did a double-take. He leaned forward, eyes wide.

Claudia approached.

From the look on his face, she knew he was impressed.

"Bite me now!" said Wyatt. "Look at you. My God, you're so beautiful."

Claudia smiled.

He leaned forward and kissed her cheek.

Claudia twirled around. "You like?"

"Yes, sir!"

She stopped twirling. "What about that dance?"

"You bet."

They headed for the dance floor. Claudia was no dancer. Once Jane had invited her clubbing, and she'd declined, telling her all she knew how to do was skate and ski.

"That's great!" Jane had said. "When on the dance floor, do the same skiing moves to the beat of the music."

That was what Claudia did now. It didn't look pretty. Her moves were not in sync with the music. Opposite her, Wyatt moved like a panther dancing to war drums. His shoulders and body were moving and twisting in sync to the beat.

The music switched to a slow one, and Claudia was now eager to escape the dance floor.

Wyatt had other ideas. His eyes bore into hers, and he wrapped his hand around her waist, pulled her closer, and kissed her. A fluttery feeling descended into Claudia's stomach.

"You've stolen my heart, Claudia Kraner."

Claudia's chest pounded with excitement. She knew he cared for her. "I never get to see you anymore."

"You will, Claudia, you will." Wyatt exhaled. "Ouch."

"Oh, sorry," said Claudia. She'd stepped on him.

"Don't worry. I'll make it up to - Ugh."

"Very sorry." She'd stepped on him again.

Claudia was relieved when the music faded toward the end. She'd stepped on his toes several times.

Wyatt whirled around as if someone had called or tapped him on the back. It was Riley, and she looked stunning.

Riley flashed Claudia a smile. "Hello, Claudia."

"Hi," said Claudia. "You look amazing."

"Thank you." Riley turned to Wyatt. "Coach, I believe I have the next dance. You promised."

Wyatt finally shut his mouth from staring at Riley. "Well...Ummm, Claudia, thanks for the dance. I promised Riley a dance." He hooked elbows with Riley, and they walked away.

Claudia was lost for words. She watched them move away, then realized she'd been abandoned on the dance floor. She'd been discarded like a tattered dishrag. She shouldn't have come back. Eyes wet and vision blurry, she walked away.

She had to get out of here yet again. As she made her way across the dance floor toward the exit, navigating through dancing sweaty bodies, she overheard a couple talking.

"Did you see the instructor, Claudia Kraner?" said the first voice. "She brought her 'A' game to this dance."

"Yeah," said the other. "But she's no match for Riley. Riley's a stunner. Stole her man from her, right here on the dance floor. Heck, if she comes my way, I'll dump you like a bad habit." The man laughed.

Claudia felt like a hand was squeezing her chest.

She couldn't breathe.

She needed air.

She burst through the exit, and the door shut behind her, cutting off the sound of music. Claudia filled her lungs. She must make a choice. Wyatt said he wanted her. But he seemed to lose his mind once Riley was around. Well, she could have him.

As she walked away, Claudia heard loud music and knew someone had exited the lounge. The door shut, cutting off the music again. Then someone called out her name.

"Claudia! Wait!"

21

CAMERON

RON HAD BEEN IN THE SHADOWS WATCHING. HE KNEW WHEN Claudia walked in. She'd changed into a dress, applied makeup, and done her hair.

She was breathtaking and as pretty as some of the women he'd worked with.

He watched her look around, and once she spotted Wyatt, her face lit up.

Wyatt!

Just like a bad penny, he always turned up. Ron had hoped the last he would see of him was in college. They had been roommates, and it hadn't ended well. Now, five years later, history was repeating itself. But this time around, it was a little different. Two women were involved, unlike one the last time.

Things had been going well between Claudia and Wyatt. They'd talked, danced, and even kissed, and then Riley showed up. Everything went south for Claudia from then on.

The despair on Claudia's face melted his heart.

He had to do something.

Her smell brought him back to the present. Clean and flowery, with a hint of spice.

"Claudia."

Claudia whirled around. Her eyebrows shot up. "Ron?" Her voice heavy with unshed tears.

"Please, wait." Ron half ran, half walked up to her. "Running away doesn't solve anything. The problem is still there when you stop running."

Claudia stared at him, as if not sure what he was talking about.

Ron took a deep breath and exhaled. "Sorry, I saw what happened in there."

Claudia whimpered. "Oh God."

"It's okay. Riley's a force of nature. Most men can't resist her when she turns on the charm."

"I thought you guys were somehow together."

Ron looked at her face. Her eyes were now brimming with tears. He glanced at a couch close to a half table. "Can we sit?"

Claudia shook her head.

"Please. I need your help, and maybe I can help you too." Ron pulled out a packet of tissues from his pocket and offered it to her.

Claudia took it. "Thank you." She extracted one and dabbed her eyes. Without answering him, she walked to the couch and sat down.

Ron sat beside her. He leaned forward, arms resting on his lap, fingers intertwined together. "Riley Carter is on her way to becoming a supermodel. I've photographed her and hundreds of other models for a while now. When it comes to makeup, fashion, presentation, Riley's learned how to put it together to her advantage. But - "

"I don't understand," said Claudia, cutting him off. "Why are you telling me all this?"

Ron sat up and raised both palms. "Please...let...let me finish. I'll get to the point quickly." He rubbed his hands together, searching his mind to find the words that won't be too devastating. "The thing is Riley has been doing this for a while now. Whether she just wants to lead Wyatt on or has feelings for him I can't tell. But she's more adept at this, and it won't be easy for you to have Wyatt looking at you without help. What I'm trying to say is, I have a plan that can help both of us achieve what we want."

Claudia cocked her head. "Okay, I'm listening."

"I've been covering Riley for a while now, and I know she's into winter sports. That's how she knew about Wyatt winning the championship competition back then. Before Riley and I arrived here, we agreed to learn together, but once Riley saw Wyatt, she couldn't contain herself. Now she thinks I'm scared of skiing and don't want to learn anymore."

"Well, I just see you taking pictures," said Claudia, not looking as despondent as before. "Is she right?"

Ron smiled. "Good question. I'm telling you this as a way for us to help each other. Wyatt and I have history. We were roommates back in college. One day my girlfriend back then told me she slept with Wyatt one weekend I'd gone home to visit my sick mom."

Claudia placed her hand on her chest. "My God, that's awful."

"Well, Wyatt was the big man on campus. Good looks, charm, skiing champion, and some youthful exuberance too."

"Yes, but..." Claudia's voice trailed off.

Ron smiled. "I was so in love with her and wished she hadn't told me. You know what they say, what you don't know won't hurt you, right? But the guilt ate her up, and once she told me, it was just a matter of time. I tried to hold it up, but the foundation had been ripped out, and eventually, we broke up."

Claudia made a *tsk* sound and shook her head. "So sorry."

Ron took a deep breath and exhaled loudly. "Okay! With that bit of information out of the way, that brings us to now. I like Riley, and I'd like to surprise her. We have a few more days before Christmas. You teach me how to ski, and I'll turn you into a supermodel."

Laughter bubbled out of Claudia. "Come on, you can't do that."

"I'll give it my best shot."

"You're not seeking revenge after all these years? I'm not Wyatt's girlfriend. We're just friends. And I wouldn't sleep with someone involved with another person either. I wouldn't like that to be done to me."

Ron laughed. "I'm not involved with Riley or seeking revenge, and we're not sleeping together. It's just to get an edge, and also help you too." Ron looked into Claudia's eyes, hesitated, then spoke. "You're beautiful. You're tall, athletic, and can ski."

They both laughed.

"You have the potential to become a supermodel. Maybe I'll discover you the way Iman, David Bowie's wife, was discovered by Peter Beard when she was a student at the University of Nairobi."

"Really? I didn't know that."

"Yeah, she's from Somalia, and Mr. Beard was in Africa taking pictures of African animals and creating journals about them when he spotted her. Her first assignment was on the cover of Vogue a year later in 1976."

"Wow," said Claudia. She tapped her lips with her fist and stared into space, deep in thought.

22

Claudia

DISCUSSING WYATT AND RILEY WITH RON HAD A SIMILAR effect on her, like when she spoke to Wyatt about her birthday. Claudia felt like a burden had been lifted off her chest.

She liked Wyatt and hoped his attraction to Riley was more of her being too in your face.

After hearing about Ron's experience with Wyatt, she came to understand more about Ron. Claudia didn't think it would be too difficult for them to work out a time to do their prep work without drawing attention. At least, the people looking for them would be engaged with each other, making it a perfect arrangement.

Claudia was excited by Ron's plan. Not about making her a supermodel, but more about learning from someone who knew the industry inside out.

Goosebumps appeared all over her skin when she thought of Iman. Just waiting at the airport to catch a plane, and a year later, you're on the cover of *Vogue* magazine. Talk about a life-changing moment. Was this her life-changing moment? More like a love-changing moment.

The sound of loud music pulled Claudia out of her thoughts. She turned to look where the sound had come from. Someone had opened the door to the lounge. A man and woman were walking away as the door shut behind them, the previous level of quietness restored.

"You've had enough time to think," said Ron with an amused look on his face. "So do we have a deal?"

"You're incorrigible. Making me a supermodel would be the icing on the cake. But that's not important. I'm more excited to see the tricks you have up your sleeve about fashion and makeup tips."

"There'll be dancing too."

Claudia's eyebrows shot up. "Dancing?"

"Of course. You were dangerous on the dance floor. I saw you. We don't want you to make your dance partner an invalid without toes by the time the dance is done."

Claudia laughed. "But it won't be easy for you either. I'm going to teach you a move that would blow Riley's socks off. If you can execute it properly, you'll blow my socks off too."

Ron nodded slowly. "You won't regret having me as a student. I'll be the best you ever had."

Claudia giggled. "It's a deal!"

She shook hands with him.

"We need a timeline. We don't want Parkinson's Law to come into play here."

Claudia's eyebrows narrowed. "Parkinson's Law? What's that?"

"Basically, means that a task expands to fill the time allotted to it."

"There's a term for that? I did not know that." Claudia clapped her hands and rubbed them vigorously as she made eye contact with Ron. "I do that all the time. Listen, the MPSR Christmas party is on the 23rd. Why don't we aim for everyone to be proficient by the 23rd?"

Ron shook his body and said, "Oh God, I'm trembling. Will I be ready?"

"You should be. You're not exactly a novice on skis. I'll have you skiing down the toughest slope here, Deer Edge, on the 24th."

"When do we start?"

Claudia was about to say *in the morning* when she remembered Max's invitation for tomorrow. She might as well go. It never hurts to follow up on a friend who is open to connecting with other people. She'd make herself scarce for the rest of the night from the resort. She was in a better mood now and didn't want to risk it by seeing any more of Wyatt or Riley tonight.

"Tomorrow?"

"I have an errand tomorrow morning. Let's play it by ear. If I'm done early, I'll call you. What's your phone number?"

They exchanged numbers.

"Thanks Ron, for everything." Claudia kissed him on the cheek. She smelled his cologne, and she felt ultra-awake as heat surged through her body.

Ron headed back to the lounge and the dance. Claudia went to her room. She didn't want anything to dampen her mood. She changed into jeans and a sweater, put on her boots, grabbed her jacket, and headed to the parking lot for her Honda Accord.

As she drove into the driveway of their cottage, she noticed the lights in Holly's house next door was on, and the Christmas decorations in the yard were up. She wondered if Holly and her family were back for Christmas already. Or had the caretaker put out the decorations? Maybe she'd check on them later. Probably easier to call Holly and find out if they were visiting.

There was no car in the driveway, but Claudia knew their Aunt Sam was visiting; maybe she went out.

The smell of homemade apple pie greeted her as soon as she stepped into the cottage. Claudia called out hello as she walked through. No one replied. She found the culprit for the aroma, an apple pie on the kitchen counter set out to cool. It also confirmed that her aunt was around and had probably stepped out.

Claudia felt a tug in her heart. The apple pie sitting on the counter was the trademark of the Tanner girls, their mother and Aunt Sam. Their aunt had laid it out just like their mother would have done. Memories were all they had left.

She went upstairs, got fresh linen from the linen closet, and continued to her room.

Claudia's room hadn't changed much since before she left for college. Her skating trophies were on one level on a book-shelf. Claudia sighed then pulled her eyes away from them. She brought out her phone and sent a text to her aunt. Told her she was around and would be leaving early in the morning for a meeting. They'd catch up later.

Claudia put her phone in airplane mode, then set her alarm for 7:00am.

23

Max

MAX SAT IN HIS TRUCK IN FOX RUN'S PARKING LOT, THE
rumble of the engine a constant in the background. It wasn't
much of a parking lot, just a flat space that could take about
three cars at a time.

He stared at the image of a fox drawn in white on a sign
with *Fox Run* underneath it. The sign was held in place with a
spike driven into the ground. Accumulated snow almost
covered the board itself. *That's probably about four feet of
snow*, thought Max. The town snow removers rarely made it
out here, and Max was glad for his truck.

He opened his thermos, and the aroma of coffee filled the
car. He always enjoyed the initial smell before his nose got
used to it. Max poured himself a cup and blew off the steam
at the top to cool it before taking a sip. Even though he
preferred his coffee with milk and sugar, he took it black
since he'd figured out that milk didn't agree with him.

He looked out of the window at the snow-covered land-scape that plunged down to the valley of sparse pine forest. Based on the almost obstructed sign, Max knew they would have a lot of snow to wade through while going up the mountain.

On the other side of that valley lay the town of Mountain Peak itself. Security lights were still on in most homes. He hoped they would be on their way before all the lights went off as the day brightened.

Max sat patiently, waiting. The heat blasting from the car's heater reminded him of other times he'd had to lay in wait for a query in a ditch under the afternoon sun in Iraq. Not only fighting the elements, but also wondering if the tingling sensation on his leg was nothing—or a poisonous viper checking him out.

Today, he had to play his cards right. Any inappropriate movement could have Claudia fleeing from him.

His mind drifted to an ambush in his army days. They would hide and lay in wait. He wondered if Claudia would show up, or if she was still in her bed wrapped up with a blanket keeping warm.

Images of that prick Wyatt wrapped up with her caused him to grip the coffee cup tighter. He didn't want to think of Claudia in that position with Wyatt, but it was a reality. Max didn't think Wyatt was right for her. He would only end up hurting her, another trophy to hang on his wall after he abandoned her. Then they…he would be left to pick up the mess.

He remembered the last woman he'd loved, and his pulse raced. No, it couldn't happen here. He was in America now. That type of outcome was very unlikely here, but still, it could happen in another form.

Max exhaled. It was just five minutes before eight. He

would wait ten minutes before he left. It would be easier to just call her and find out where she was. But if she didn't answer, that would only make him more anxious.

He wondered if Claudia had gotten over her infatuation for him. Whether the childhood crush was now gone and replaced hopefully by a physical attraction. Before he knew it, he was having a conversation inside his head with two versions of himself.

Don't be a moron, said one version. *If she didn't like you, she wouldn't be coming out to the mountains with you.*

Duh, so you think she likes you. Where is she? said the second version.

Max stopped thinking and looked at the back of the truck, at the backpack he would be bringing up. Maybe he should start to line it up. His military training hadn't left him yet.

In a war zone, sticking to your schedule could be the difference between life and death. For him, leaving in ten minutes meant precisely that. He'd brought extra jackets, boots, and snowshoes in different sizes in case she forgot.

The time on his dash said he had only two minutes left before his take-off time. He tossed back his coffee, grimaced at the lukewarm bitter taste, then put his hat and gloves on. He stretched out over to the back seat and crossed-checked all he would be carrying. He was ready. Moments later, he looked at the time on his dash. It was now twelve minutes after eight, two minutes over his departure time.

Even though going to see the old man was fun, bringing Claudia was the main attraction. He'd give her another three minutes, he said to himself. It was very uncharacteristic of him, but every rule has an exception, he rationalized to himself.

Max had backed into the parking lot. He leaned to the

backseat and slipped the thermos into a side pocket. When Max looked up, he froze. His pulse beat faster. Approaching him was the headlights of a car. As the vehicle turned, he saw it was a Honda. A car he associated with the Kraner girls. Heat flushed through his body; Claudia was here.

24

Claudia

CLAUDIA HEARD THE CRUNCHING OF SNOW AS SHE DROVE OFF the main road towards Max's car. Between setting her alarm and putting her phone in airplane mode, something had gone wrong, and the alarm didn't go off to wake her up. Luckily, her internal alarm had. She showered fast, got dressed, and was about to make a beeline for the exit when her aunt appeared from the kitchen.

Aunt Sam was a young-looking forty-something, and Claudia and her sisters related well with her. She must have seen that Claudia was running late and backed away.

"Hi, Sam. Bye, Sam!" said Claudia with a smile. "I have to run - going hiking with Max Steel."

"In this weather? Have fun, bye. I'll send you a text."

They'd greeted each other quickly before Claudia rushed outside and took off in the Honda.

As Claudia parked her car beside Max's, she hoped he

was still there and hadn't left without her. That would be disastrous. She glanced at the snowy forest. There was no way she would risk going in there on her own. She cursed herself again for waking up late. Then she noticed the puff of air coming from the truck's exhaust just as the door opened and Max stepped out.

He waved at her.

Claudia killed the engine and ran out. "Hey! Sorry I'm late. My alarm, for some reason, didn't go off. I'm so happy you waited." She ran to him and hugged him. He smelled of coffee and expensive cologne—one of those ones with blue in their name. Things were suddenly looking great for Claudia. She had a guy who would teach her about fashion, and here was another taking her sight-seeing.

Claudia looked around and wondered why anyone in their right mind would go hiking in the snow without company. There was no way she would ever be caught dead here alone. What if she got lost? Right now, she trusted Max. She knew she was in safe hands with him.

"I have coffee," said Max with a big grin on his face.

"No, we're already running late, thanks to me. I'll have some when we get there." Claudia paused. She hadn't asked many questions about where they were going because what girl doesn't like surprises? This was the time to clear any lingering doubts. "How far is it, time-wise?"

Max placed his backpack on the snow. "Probably thirty, maybe forty minutes. Mostly depends on the snow. It's dry right now, so it shouldn't be challenging." He reached into the back seat of the truck, came up, and held up something. "Ever used one of these before?"

"Are those snowshoes?"

"Yep, I know," said Max, nodding. "They look different from the ones you're used to."

"Those look like shoes on a short ski slide. The ones we had as kids looked like tennis rackets."

"Everything is getting a makeover these days. Distributes your weight so that you don't have to sink into the snow and spend energy pulling your feet out with each step."

Claudia's fascination with the snowshoes was fleeting. Her eyes were on Max as he spoke. He fascinated her. He looked confident and capable, and she wondered what it would feel like to be locked in his wild embrace. Max's voice drew her out of her reverie.

"Claudia?"

"Oops, sorry. What did you say again?"

"Here," said Max, thrusting the snowshoes at her. "Don't fall asleep on me here with your eyes wide open. Were you daydreaming? With my arms locked around you in a passionate embrace?"

Claudia's nostrils flared. Heat rushed through her body. How did he know? She bent down and started to put on the snowshoes so he wouldn't see her flustered look. She took a few quick breaths to calm herself, then got up. "So, who's this old guy we're going to see?"

Max slung his backpack on his back, clicked the strap around his waist, and glanced at Claudia. "Ready?"

"I was born ready!" said Claudia with attitude.

Max made a fist with both hands, leaned back, and growled. "Yeah!"

They both started to laugh.

"Come on, I'll tell you as we walk."

Claudia walked behind Max. It was an easy start. The snowshoes made walking awkward, but she noticed the difference it made.

"When I was a kid, I loved to explore the woods, just like most kids around here. My grandparents raised me after my parents died, and they believed kids should be left to roam around on their own. They grew up in a different era and had a different mindset."

"Like free-range chicken," injected Claudia.

"Exactly. It was fun back then, until one day, I got lost."

Claudia brought her gloved hands together in front of her mouth. "Oh no."

"Yeah. Initially, I wasn't scared. I just didn't know where I was. But I could retrace my footprints on the snow, easy."

Claudia continued walking right behind Max. They were just a few feet apart. "Let me guess, it started snowing?"

"Bingo!"

They walked on. Sometimes, Max would stop talking as they navigated the terrain, then continue when they passed the challenging part. They'd been walking for about fifteen minutes when Max spoke again.

"Turn around here."

"Whoa!" The scene below was the whole town laid out. "That's breathtaking." Claudia looked around some more. "There's our cottage!"

"You can only see this far in winter. In summer, the trees are blooming, and their leaves block the view."

Claudia brought out her camera and took a few shots. In the distance, she could see the neighboring town too.

"Okay, let's continue," said Max.

"So what happened to you after you got lost?"

"It got dark quickly. I wasn't scared of animals getting me. The bears were hibernating. We don't have wolves here. But you never know. It was the cold and the snow; it kept on coming down. I smelled the smoke first. Smells are like sound; they travel far. And sometimes you don't know how close or far you are to the source." Max turned back and looked at Claudia. "Do you want to take a break?"

"How much farther do we have to go?"

"Maybe another twenty minutes."

It was just cold. The faster they got there, the sooner they'd be out of the cold. "Let's keep on going."

"Anyway, to cut the story short, the snow kept on coming down, and eventually it got so deep that I couldn't even move. That's how I learned about snowshoes. I never used to like them. So, his name is Brad Bradford. He has a dog who's also named Bradford. The dog found me. Otherwise, I would have turned into a Popsicle."

They reached the summit and walked down a few feet on the other side of the mountain. Claudia noticed the absence of a town in the valley on this side of the hill; it was all wilderness. A few feet below was a flat expanse with a log cabin.

"We've arrived," said Max.

"That's beautiful! You know all the picture-perfect spots. Can I take a picture?" Claudia reached into her pocket again. The snow was undisturbed. No footprints, and the cabin's windows glowed yellow.

"Sure, go ahead. I'm sure Bradford wouldn't mind."

Claudia took a few shots.

"He's a recluse. This is the first time I'm bringing anyone to see him."

Claudia stopped and looked at Max. "Did you ask him before bringing me? I've read about recluses. They value their privacy."

"Hold your horses. I told him I would be coming with someone special."

Claudia tilted her head. "Who's the special person? You only brought me."

Max pointed at Claudia.

Claudia whirled around. Nobody. She turned around to face Max, eyebrows knitted together. Then it dawned on her.

A smile tugged one corner of her lip. "Oh." She lowered her head, the frown replaced with a smile.

"Both of you cut it out!" said a gruff voice. "You get to your final destination, then start to argue. Come on in!"

25

Claudia

THE SMELL OF ANIMAL FAT, WOODSMOKE, AND OLD DOG greeted them once they entered the log cabin. It was a welcome relief from the cold outside, with a big fireplace with a massive fire going. Inside Bradford's cabin was what Claudia imagined walking into Hagrid's cottage in Harry Potter would feel like - hot.

There was no TV, in fact no electricity, and Claudia wondered how the old man passed the time. She didn't have to wonder for long. A comfortable-looking bed with blankets lay on the opposite side of the fireplace, next to a round wooden table with three chairs. A rocking chair with an open book placed on the cushion was placed close to the bed. More books lay on the shelf, and Claudia didn't have to imagine any longer how the old man spent time here. Sleeping and reading were excellent ways to kill time.

An old Lab lay on a rug close to the fire. It didn't move when they entered, nor did it raise its head when Claudia came closer to hang her jacket on a coat rack next to it. Claudia looked at Bradford, eyebrows raised, wondering if everything was okay.

Bradford was jovial. "He's definitely doing better than me," he said with a deep resonating voice and waved a hand in dismissal. "Ho ho ho." He rubbed his hand over his enormous belly covered with a white collarless long-sleeved tee shirt. "At least he gets to sleep all day, a feat I can't achieve."

Claudia liked him at first sight. Bradford had the laugh and girth, all he needed was a red hat, red cloak with white trimmings, and he would pass for Santa Claus. She wouldn't be surprised if there was a barn close by with a herd of reindeer feeding on hay, waiting for Christmas Eve.

"What was so important that you two had to stop in front of my cabin to vent?" asked Bradford as he threw on some steak and fish onto a skillet over a charcoal fire.

Heat coursed through Claudia's body, despite the high temperature inside the cabin. She wanted to shout out because Max thought she was special. Instead, she kept her head down.

The steak and fish, plus pickled onions and peppers Bradford served, were among the most delicious dishes Claudia had ever had.

Bradford had been around for a long time and seemed to know everything about Mountain Peak.

Bradford stuffed his pipe with tobacco after the meal. As he enjoyed his smoke, Max had coffee, while Claudia waited for the water to get ready for hot chocolate.

"From my vantage point up here," said Bradford, puffing at his pipe, "I saw the town grow and spread over the years."

He remembered the Eastmans, Claudia's former neighbors. He used to guide their great-grandfather on bear and deer hunting trips when he was a boy himself.

"Max, you've hit the jackpot with this lass. She's beautiful. Reminds me of a damsel I saw one of the many times I went off the Appalachian Trail. I was going to make her Mrs. Bradford until her papa showed up in the barn and introduced me to the cold double barrel of his gun. He'd crept up and pressed it against my butt. I became the gent in distress and ran like hell."

Claudia nearly choked on her hot chocolate made with water from melted snow.

Enthralled by old Bradford's dazzling tales and the flickering flames from the fireplace illuminating Max Steel's handsome face, Claudia wished the day would never end. She'd never seen Max so relaxed and happy. It was easily the happiest and most enjoyable few hours she'd had in a long time.

"Come on Claudia, it's time we hit the trail back," said Max, smiling. "I don't have a double-barrel to keep him away if he makes a move on you and decides to make you Mrs. Bradford."

"Oh, you're leaving already? I was just starting with my stories."

Claudia looked at Max. "We'll be back again, right? I really had fun."

"Claudia, you're welcome anytime. I'll be spending Christmas with my sister at the Poconos this year. But I don't have to be here for you to visit and enjoy the cabin. The key is always hidden in the birdfeeder."

Claudia got up from her chair and went to get her coat. The dog opened its eyes, looked at her, and then closed one. "He winked at me!" yelled Claudia.

"What?" yelled Bradford. "It takes a beautiful woman to get him to open his eyes. That dog!"

Max laughed. "Well, old-timer thanks so much for having us."

"Anytime."

They put on their coats and snowshoes.

Max put the now empty backpack relieved of canned food, books, and medicine on his back and Bradford placed a hand on Max's shoulder as they approached the door. "Son, she's a keeper. I see happiness in your future, a happy and perfect union."

"Thank you, sir," said Max.

"Hope to see you again soon, and thanks for the lovely time," said Claudia.

Well rested, Claudia stepped out for the return journey full of energy. She felt safe and happy, and she appreciated the scenery as if seeing it for the first time. She had this hyper-awareness in her because of Max's closeness. It was like experiencing Nirvana.

"We'll make a little deviation," said Max. "There's something I want to share with you."

With the sound of her heartbeat loud in her ears, Claudia followed. *We can make as many deviations as you want,* she thought. The good thing about the return trip is it's always faster. But today, Claudia would rather have it slow to a crawl. She was surprised when she noticed familiar landmarks they'd passed on their way up. She didn't know they were so close to where they'd parked the cars.

Max took her hand.

Despite her hands being gloved, Claudia felt a jolt of electricity rush through her body. She was in high school again, when just holding hands was the height of her intimate experience.

Max pointed at a mountain ridge view. "Claudia, I've

known you forever, but right now, I feel I really know you... I don't know how else to explain it."

Claudia knew what he meant. She felt the same in her heart. In the distance, the red glow of twilight was an exhibition of colors. Claudia felt an incredible urge to do something. She reached up, grabbed Max's head, and pulled him down. Their lips met, and soon they were kissing like their lives depended on it.

"Oh God, Claudia! You possessed my soul from the first time I saw you."

Claudia's pulse raced. They kissed some more, then broke off.

"The cars are not far," said Max. His voice was tight with want. He took Claudia's hands, and they walked back hand in hand.

They stumbled into the truck.

"It's even colder than outside," said Claudia.

Max turned the ignition and cranked the heater up. He pressed down on the accelerator, hoping to rev up the engine and get the car warmer faster. He took off the backpack and tossed it to the back.

Claudia was on fire. She was breathing hard and could see the fog cloud each time she exhaled. Was this the time to have mad monkey sex? They started to kiss again, and right at that moment, Claudia knew it was love that she felt. Claudia couldn't tell if the car was now heating up or molten lava was flowing through her veins. One thing was for sure: he'd set her aflame. She was burning up and had never wanted anyone as much as she wanted him.

Without warning, Max pulled back. "I...I can't."

Claudia's eyes widened. She couldn't believe it. It was just like that night outside the lounge. "Max, you did it again!"

"We…we have to - "

"What?" Claudia stared at him with shock and disbelief. Was it her? What did she do? "You know what - whatever!" She opened the door, got out, and slammed it shut. She got into her Honda and pushed the ignition button. The car came on, then spluttered and died. She tried the ignition again, and all she heard was a click. Claudia pushed the ignition button repeatedly until even the click ceased. "No, no, no." She slammed her fist on the steering wheel, teeth clenched.

Max opened Claudia's door.

Claudia jumped, looked at him, then turned her head to the other side.

"I…I think the battery is dead." Max reached for the hood release button, then drew back. "I'll…I'll jump you. Let me get the cable from my trunk." He walked away, his feet crunching in the snow.

Claudia looked in the rearview mirror and noticed tears streaming down her cheeks. She pulled off her gloves and wiped them. She was frustrated and confused. What was going on here? It must be her. What did she do wrong? Everything was-

"I think my jumper cable is at home. Let's go get it."

Claudia waved him away, not bothering to look at him.

"I can't do that, Claudia. You'll freeze to death just sitting in your car."

Maybe she was better off dead. Claudia knew he was right. She got out of the car, never looking at him, and climbed into the passenger side. She was done with him.

Max said, "I'm sorry for - "

"Please," said Claudia with her finger raised as she continued to gaze out of her window.

They drove in silence.

Max turned on the radio. The Christmas song *Joy to the World* blared from the speakers.

Claudia turned it off. There was no joy here.

Max looked at her, his mouth open. He closed it and refocused on the road. The only sound in the car was the *click click click* of the turn signal.

They arrived at his home, which was about ten minutes from Fox Run Ridge.

"Why don't you come inside while I look for the jumper cables?"

Claudia said nothing.

Max shrugged. "Okay." He walked away, unlocked the front door, and entered, leaving it slightly open.

Claudia watched as lights came on in the ranch-style house. The more she looked, the more anger boiled in her. *Who does he think he is?* She worked herself into a frenzy, and before she knew it, she was out of the car, heading toward the house.

Claudia stepped into the living room, yanking off her gloves as she looked around—leather couches, a flat-screen TV on the wall, a fireplace with a fire already going. On the fireplace mantel was a framed picture of a younger Max in army camouflage. Claudia's breath caught. That was the version she'd dreamed of for so many years. Then she heard footsteps, and Max appeared with jumper cables in his hands.

He grinned. "You came in." He raised the cables. "I found them."

In two steps, Claudia stood in front of Max and-*whack,* slapped him on the cheek.

"Why do you do that to me all the time? You think I didn't know what you did to me on the sleigh? Squeezing me. Feeling me up, then pretending nothing happened. Why? You lure me in. You know I care for you, then you bait and switch."

Max remained quiet.

"Say something." Tears streamed down her face.

Whack.

She hit him across the face again.

Max blurted, "I don't want to hurt you, okay?"

"What nonsense! Hurt me? How? Are you a serial killer?" She raised her hand to slap him again.

This time Max caught it.

She looked into his eyes, and they were on fire. Claudia knew Max would never hurt her. But she'd crossed a line. And when you cross a line, there are consequences.

Max's lips were a thin line. A deep animal growl escaped his throat. In one swift move, he gripped her hands together with one large hand. With the other, he wound the cable over her wrists and bound them together.

Claudia's mouth went dry.

She sensed her insides vibrating.

26

Claudia

CLAUDIA'S BREATH HITCHED.

Her heartbeat galloped like wild horses in her chest.

She glared at him, her eyes as wide as saucers. *Sweet Jesus, what have I gotten myself into?*

Max stared at her, then leaned closer as if she were his favorite cake, and he was wondering which part to bite off first.

Now they were breathing the same air. Max brushed his lips against hers, tugging and taking small bites.

Claudia felt her insides turn to liquid. Each time their lips made contact, she stuck out her tongue and tried to lick him. He pulled back.

Max brushed her hair with his fingers, massaging her scalp. He wound a hank of blond hair around his fist and yanked.

Claudia felt a sharp pain as her hair stretched at the roots.

He tilted her head backward, and his mouth found hers. Pain and pleasure collided in her head.

Max walked the fine line between pain and pleasure. This time he wasn't teasing anymore. His tongue probed her mouth, and she responded, her tongue coming out to play.

Claudia's knees turned to jelly. She could barely stand. She didn't notice when he unwrapped his hand from her hair and travel down to her jeans, unbuckled them, and slid over the top into her panties. She gasped when his fingers brushed past her pubic hair and landed on her core. She was soaking wet.

Max brought out his finger and stuck it into his mouth.

Watching him lick her juices set her on fire anew.

"I'm going to take off your jacket and strip you naked. If you want me to stop, tell me when."

Oh, God, her body was shaking. She'd wanted him forever. Claudia knew she wasn't going to tell him to stop. She nodded. Right away, she felt her jacket come off her shoulders. He unbuttoned her sweater, exposing her bra. Max tried to remove her sweater and jacket, but her hands were tied together.

"Fuck." Max lifted her bra cups, and her breasts spilled out. He looked at them greedily, then lowered his head and took one nipple into his mouth. He did the same to the other nipple. He raised his head and found her eyes on him, watching, wanting him.

"Are…are you going to fuck me?" Claudia asked, raising her bound wrists.

"No, you are going to ride me."

Max placed his palm between her breasts and gave her a gentle shove. Claudia landed on the leather couch behind her.

Max took off her boots and socks. He reached for her hips and peeled off her jeans. His hands reached down, grabbed her ankles, and placed her feet on the couch. He was on his knees, her pussy at eye level with his face.

Is he going to eat it? Claudia quivered with anticipation. Her thighs spasmed when Max ran a finger along her inner thighs and followed that up with his tongue tracing a wet path down her thigh. He sucked the middle of her thigh, getting a moan from her. He did the same for her other thigh, and when his lips finally settled on her core, Claudia thought she'd died and gone to heaven.

Max worked on her lips, tugging and pulling.

But Claudia wanted his cock inside her. "My turn." She got off the couch, unbuttoned his shirt, and removed it with his jacket. Max pulled his T-shirt over his head, and Claudia gasped when she saw the scars on his well-sculpted torso.

"Battle scars," said Max. "They don't hurt anymore."

Claudia bit his nipples one after the other, causing him to suck in air each time.

With her hands still tied at the wrist, she reached down, unbuckled his jeans, and slid them and his boxers to his ankles as she dropped to her knees.

His cock sprang free. Thick, long, and hard. Claudia swallowed. She wanted to wrap her mouth around it.

He stepped out of his jeans and boxers just as she shoved him.

Max grinned as he landed on the couch. His cock leaned to one side, like the Tower of Pisa, pulsating with every beat of his heart.

Claudia raked her nails down his body and grabbed his cock. The fullness of his cock in her hands caused her to gasp.

Max shut his eyes and groaned, thoroughly enjoying himself.

Claudia stared at his square jaw, two-day-old stubble, and the flaring of his nostrils as she stroked his cock.

Max opened his eyes and stared at her. "You don't have to fuck me if you don't want. Sometimes, wanting something is better than having it."

"I know. But I'm going to fuck you. I've wanted to for a long time." She continued to stroke his cock. "Why did you tie my wrists?"

Max lifted his palms and let them drop on the couch. "I don't know. You were behaving like an unruly child, and I thought I'd teach you a lesson." He shrugged and tried to get up. "Let me untie you."

Claudia placed both palms on his rock-hard abs and pushed him back. "No. The anticipation and not knowing was exciting." She put his cock in a chokehold with her left hand and rubbed the tip with her right.

Max's abs tightened, and a deep moan escaped his throat. Claudia got up from the floor, placed her bound hands over his neck, and straddled him. She tried to guide his cock in by maneuvering her hip, but couldn't get it in. Max tried to help.

"No hands," blurted Claudia. "I can do this."

Max obeyed.

On the third try, they both gasped as Max's cock slid into where it needed to go.

Max's hands settled on either side of her hips, rolled over her butt cheeks, then went underneath. He lifted her up, then slammed her down the length of his shaft.

A sharp breath rushed out of Claudia as he raised her again and slammed her down. Jolts of pleasure coursed through her body as new hands and a new foreign body buried deep inside her sent new sensations all over her body. The thought that she'd slept with two guys in less than a week thrilled her compared to her last record of two in what-five years?

Max let go of her hips.

She just sat there with his cock buried deep inside her, her eyes on his face. Claudia clenched her muscles and squeezed his cock. She laughed as his eyes widened.

"How did you do that?"

Claudia squeezed his cock again and bit her lower lip.

Max threw his head back and moaned. "You're a keeper."

"I haven't even begun yet." Claudia started to move and rock her hips.

Faster.

Deeper.

Max's breathing came in gasps.

His living room was already as hot as Bradford's home. Now, with Claudia on top, it was sizzling.

Sweat dripped from her forehead onto her chest. Claudia wanted to moan, shout, and speak of how much fun she was having. Her first attempt at speaking was a word salad. She bit her lower lips to stop from being vocal. But she couldn't help herself. She pumped and ground on Max, his hands holding her ass like an oversized beach ball.

Since she'd started to ride him, his mouth had hung open in a big O, inhaling and exhaling. The leather couch groaned under the assault. Max's grunts and her moans were the only other sounds in the room. The smell of his cologne mixed with sweat was like an aphrodisiac. Claudia rode him faster.

As if to distract himself, Max leaned forward, took a nipple in his mouth, and started to suck on it.

Claudia refused to be ignored and worked him harder, pressing her pelvis into his and grinding her clit against him. At the rate she was going, she was surprised he hadn't come yet. She was not going to wait for him. She'd already waited a lifetime. She felt her orgasm catch and started to whimper.

Max reached for her clit, stroking as fast as he could to get her to her destination.

Claudia plastered her body against his bare sweaty chest. She arched her back as a combination of his cock buried deep inside her and his finger working overtime sent her over the edge.

She lay against his chest, moaning, trying to catch her breath, tasting his salty sweat through her open mouth.

Her respite was short-lived.

Soon, Max had her on her knees and elbows on the couch, butt in the air.

He had one hand on each hip, drawing her toward him and then away as his cock slid in and out. He was fucking her hard, chasing his own release, filling the room with the *slap slap slap* of skin against skin.

Claudia couldn't believe it as she found herself on the pinnacle again, and within seconds crashed over the edge. Her second orgasm left her whimpering and drained.

With a deep, masculine groan, Max found his release.

His hands tightened on her butt. Nails dug into her skin, and he shook like a leaf caught in a strong gust of wind.

27

Claudia

CLAUDIA DROVE DOWNHILL TOWARD MAIN STREET. MAX HAD turned off while they were driving down and headed home. He had wanted to follow her all the way to the lodge to make sure the car got home in one piece, but she demurred.

Claudia felt so good inside and outside. Max had warned her that sometimes anticipation was better than receiving. For her, getting fucked by him was even better than any thoughts of what it could have been. She relished the moment again in her mind, going through every step.

After they caught their breaths, he'd untied her wrist, and she'd removed her sweater and jacket. Since they were still naked, the tools of the trade out there and handy, they had sex again. The second time, it was lovemaking.

They started from that same couch, then moved to the rug on the floor. Soon, Claudia was on her back with Max sliding in and out and Claudia working underneath him, writhing and moaning.

Then he'd lifted her up and carried her, with his cock still buried inside her, to the dining table. Claudia believed it was a fantasy he was fulfilling. She didn't mind at all. She got to look him in his face, look in his eyes, and watch his lips move as he came inside her, calling out her name because of what she was doing to him.

It took another hour before they got back to her car. As Max connected the jumper cable to his truck battery, Claudia was surprised to find herself getting aroused. She knew she would never see a jumper cable in the same way after being bound with it.

Finally, her car started after a few tries, and Max said to let it run for a few minutes before driving off.

"The battery is probably old," Max had said. "Needs to be changed."

"I need a new one?" she asked, not knowing the history of the car's maintenance. Nicole had left it at the house after she got married. Dad had sold his car before moving to Florida, so it was the cottage car for anyone in the house to make use of.

"Yes. A battery in good shape should start the car even if the inside light was left on for a few hours. You can spend the night with me, and we'll get it taken care of tomorrow."

Claudia would have gladly stayed the weekend, but when she checked her phone for the time, she noticed that she'd never switched off the airplane mode. When she finally turned it off, there was an avalanche of text messages. From Aunt Sam, her friend Jane, Wyatt, and several from Ron.

"Oh, Ron."

"What was that?" asked Max.

"I promised to help Ron—Cameron—with his skiing."

"Isn't he already signed up? He has an instructor, right?"

"It's a long story. He wants to impress Riley." Claudia

couldn't tell him her own part of the deal. God, she'd fucked two different men in less than a week. She was becoming a slut.

Max's lips moved as if he wanted to ask more questions, then he obviously thought better of it.

They drove off, and as they approached Max's turn-off, he honked, stuck his hand out the window, and waved.

Claudia honked and waved back. Her phone chirped, bringing her back from her reminiscing. She looked down at it. It was another text from Wyatt asking her where she was.

"Jealous, are we now?" said Claudia out loud. She sent a text to Ron. They could start skiing tomorrow morning if it was okay with him. She put the phone down and continued toward the lodge. Wyatt she would see whenever.

Claudia got to the lodge, and luck was on her side. She went straight to her room, and the only people she encountered on the way were a couple she didn't know. She got to her room, took a hot shower, and got into bed.

Before she dozed off, she sent a text to Max, telling him she had gotten back safely, and she'd had a wonderful time. And would love to get together again soon.

28

CAMERON

RON STOOD CLOSE TO THE SKI LIFT DRESSED IN LAYERS TO keep the cold away. It was early in the morning, and the sun was not yet up to warm up the air. So far, he was losing the battle. Nobody else was around, and he wanted to start skiing before the slope got busy.

He hoped Claudia would appear soon so they could get the training underway. He knew for sure that once he was engaged in some activity, he would be less cold.

He'd been glad when Claudia sent him a text last night. Before then, he'd thought their plan had all been in vain. Ron wasn't exactly sure what was going on between Riley and Wyatt. But unless Wyatt had changed, the Wyatt he knew would have fucked Riley a long time ago once she showed interest in him.

Being a photographer, working with models day in and out exposed Ron to a wide range of people and made him a better judge of character.

Riley, he believed, sometimes sent out misleading signals. She also had a reputation for throwing herself into things intensely, especially with activities like skiing. She would use her feminine wiles to get her way. Skiing was a skill you attained for yourself, but you could get someone to train you by being yourself.

Ron couldn't in all honesty say where he was with Riley. He would try his best to win her over. If he could impress her with skiing, then he would have a chance. If it didn't work out, at least he would have gotten better at it.

Ron looked around. Where was Claudia? He hoped she wasn't sleeping in. Maybe she'd forgotten about their rendezvous. He did a few jumping jacks to keep warm, then looked toward the lodge, hoping he would see her coming. Negative.

The wind shifted, and the smell of sausages and bacon drifted up to him. His stomach rumbled, and he wished he had eaten something before coming out.

Ron glanced at the ski slopes and wished he'd been diligent with his practice the coach had assigned to him, instead of hanging around Riley all the time, taking pictures and getting annoyed with her antics with Wyatt.

A sound behind him drew his attention. He whirled around. In the distance, he saw a figure in sky blue overalls coming down the slope. The skiing was perfect. Gracious to watch. He wondered when he would ski that fast and have the control he needed not to crash into a tree. Who could it be?

To his surprise, the figure came swooshing toward him. The skiing was so graceful that he just stood and watched, unabashed, forgetting his own predicament. The skier came closer and closer, and coming to a halt in front of him, sprayed him with snow.

Ron smiled, brushed snow off his jacket, and said, "Nice

skiing." He looked toward the lodge again, hoping that Claudia would show up to start his training.

The figure dug his or her ski poles into the snow and removed the ski goggles.

"Claudia!" Ron shook his head. "I should have known."

Claudia smiled.

"I expected you to be coming from the lodge."

Claudia's chest rose and fell as she tried to catch her breath. "Hi." She sounded breathless. "That could be you in a few days."

"Thanks so much for coming. I thought…well, I thought you changed your mind."

"No, it's not one-sided. I'm curious too. I want to see what you have to offer in terms of fashion."

Ron pointed at the ski lift. "I don't know where the operator went. How did you get up there?"

"Oh, I hitched a ride with one of the maintenance guys on their snowmobile. It's not too bad, we'll walk up. Hopefully, by the time we get down, the lift should be operational."

Ron nodded. "I'm ready."

Claudia laughed. "Let me catch my breath first. This is not a contest."

"Right."

Claudia took off her skis, rested for a few minutes to recover fully, and said, "Let's go."

"Are you sure? There's no rush."

"No, it's too early to take a nap," said Claudia giggling. "Grab your skis."

They started to walk up the gentle slope.

"Busy day yesterday?"

"Kind of. I went home as soon as we finished talking Friday night."

"Where's home?" asked Ron as they trudged along on the snow.

"Mountain Peak."

Ron stopped. "What? You grew up here?"

Claudia smiled and nodded. "What about you?"

"Levittown, Long Island." They continued to walk. A few moments later, Ron spoke. "So who was home? You ran back to Mommy?"

Before the past 8th of December, such a question would have felt like poking needles into her heart. But because of Wyatt's intervention, she now saw it differently. "No. Actually, only my aunt on my mom's side was there. Dad retired to Florida a couple of years ago. My sisters are both married and live elsewhere. Nicole, the eldest, lives in Massachusetts. They have a vacation home next to our cottage. Holly lives in California. They might come around too. She and her husband are building a Christmas resort a few towns away from here." Claudia exhaled. "And our mother died some years ago on my birthday."

Ron stopped walking. "My God," rushed out of him in a whisper. "I'm so sorry."

"It's all right now. I just have - "

"Jesus, you must have had shitty birthdays from that day on." Ron dropped his skis on the ground. He went to Claudia and wrapped his arms around her. He knew exactly how she felt.

Claudia giggled, her hands beside her holding on to her gear. "Okay, Ron, let's go. If I didn't know you well, I would have thought you were taking advantage of my sorrow to feel me up."

Ron let her go and stepped back. "Sorry, no. I know exactly how you feel. My father, in a drunken, jealous rage, shot my mother and then himself, because she was leaving him after my birthday party. I was ten. But from then onward, each time my birthday came up, it was torture."

Claudia's skis and poles fell to the snow in several thuds. Her hands now free, she hugged him back and rubbed his back. After about ten seconds, Claudia tapped him on the back. "All right, let's go. We have work to do."

Ron picked up his skis. "My birthday is on July 14th. When is yours?"

"Mine just passed. December 8th."

"Darn, I missed it." Ron's pulse raced. "I wish we'd come earlier. Someone that understands what you're going through would make a difference." Heat radiated through his chest. Ron felt like he'd known Claudia forever. "I'll never miss your birthday."

Claudia laughed. "I can't promise the same, but I'll call when I remember."

"Good enough."

For the rest of the morning, they went up and down the slopes practicing. Ron was determined to learn. They took a break for lunch in the afternoon. During the break, since Claudia had grown up in Mountain Peak, Ron decided on a dancing studio in the next town, so that Wyatt or Riley wouldn't stumble on to them.

Later in the evening, it was Ron's turn to coach Claudia. And because she'd mentioned the incident with her car battery, they dropped it off at a garage. Claudia paid in full, telling them they would pick it up on their way back.

The partner dancing practice was for one hour. From there, they went to the mall in that town and looked at dresses and fashion accessories.

"I like this dress," said Claudia at one of the shops.

Ron looked at it. "For somebody else. It would hang like

a curtain on you. You need something to show those curves of yours."

Claudia blushed. "Curves?"

"Yes, you've got plenty."

"No, I'm skinny."

"Nope. Toned with curves in all the right places."

Ron found himself taking pictures of her too, while skiing, modeling, and dancing. He was slowly building a portfolio of photos of her, and another in his heart and mind.

He knew every contour of her face. He could tell when she was happy or sad. In fact, she'd possessed his soul.

For the next couple of days, they would get up early and practice before anybody was up. Then Claudia would do her coaching for the day, and Ron would take a few pictures of Riley with Wyatt, and then practice with his assigned instructors. In the evenings, he met up with Claudia at the dance studio, and from there they went to the mall.

Riley didn't seem to notice he wasn't always there. That was fine with him and Claudia. The more time Riley and Wyatt were together, the more he learned from Claudia. The way he saw it, if anything was going on between Wyatt and Riley, it was already advanced. If not, he still had a chance to make an impact.

29

Max

MAX READ HER TEXT AND EXHALED. CLAUDIA HAD GOTTEN back to the lodge safely without incident.

The unexpected release of tension he'd felt slowly faded. Max hadn't planned on sleeping with her. He had tried to dissuade her with that quote about it being better to want than to receive. But she would have none of it.

He was in his living room sitting on the same couch they'd made love on. The TV was on, showing a Christmas themed shopping ad. Just thinking of her got him hard. The quote had been for himself. He'd fucked her, yet he still yearned for her. It was a physical and spiritual need rolled into one. She completed him, made him whole.

Then there was the other part he didn't want to expose her to. When people got close to him, something terrible always happened to them. Should he tell her? She might get hurt and feel that he'd had his way with her, and then gave a reason just to dump her. That would devastate her, and he didn't want to hurt her.

What if she harmed herself? Max sat up straight. Where would that leave him? Keeping away could possibly be the best he could do to save her. What was he going to do?

30

Claudia

CLAUDIA LEFT THE LODGE AND HEADED FOR THE SLOPES where she knew Ron would be. He was an eager student and definitely wanted to impress Riley. Dressed in layers as usual, with a shell jacket as the top layer, she'd placed a cap over her head to hold her hair in place and put on her gloves.

Claudia didn't have any gear to carry because Ron insisted he would bring it. She'd refused initially, but he always stole them at the end of the day and took them with him in the mornings. She trudged along, her mind drifting to the events of the past several days.

Claudia smiled as she realized it was the twenty-second of December, and she was to graduate the next day, the 23rd, the night of the Christmas party. Ron would graduate on Christmas Eve, leaving Christmas Day open for people to do whatever they wanted. And those going to leave. Most vacationers stayed on to the New Year.

"Wow," Claudia said to herself as she headed up the slope toward Ron. "Time does fly when you're having fun."

She hadn't seen Max Steel since the day they'd had monkey sex. He was still actively running the instructors, but she'd never set eyes on him since that night. He hadn't returned her texts and calls either, but she'd lumped it all up as Max being Max. He was avoiding her and making himself scarce again.

The other reason why their paths hadn't crossed was that she'd been getting up early to meet with Ron. When they were done after about two hours or so of skiing, she would go straight to her coaching assignment for the day. It could be skiing, snowboarding, or skating. She always had the schedule.

Wyatt was still coaching Riley, which sometimes left Claudia confused. It was as if Wyatt wasn't sure what he wanted—Claudia or Riley.

Claudia was convinced Wyatt had the hots for Riley, but he still wanted Claudia. He wanted to eat his cake and have it. Claudia always claimed to be busy when he wanted to meet. She was busy prepping with Ron, and they barely had enough time. All her free time was spent with Ron. She hoped to dazzle by the 23rd.

Jane and her boyfriend were back, which had helped offset the demand for practice sessions. A few more instructors were brought on board, too, and seemed to help.

Claudia raised her head and sniffed. She'd reached a part of the landscape where a draft from the kitchen often always passed through. This morning she smelled freshly baked bread.

The resort now looked like a colony of penguins full to the brim. Most of Claudia's classes were full, and more and more people were on the premises. Families from all over the world, Europe, Africa, Asia, the Middle East, South America, Australia, you name it, were represented, trying their best to have a good time and enjoy the holidays.

She could see Ron at the top of the slope, and he waved at her. Ron was an eager student, and she was surprised by how fast he picked up new skills. Sometimes he wanted to outdo himself, but she always tried to have him focus on his mission, which was to learn enough to impress Riley, not break a bone, or perhaps his neck too.

"When are we going to ski Devils Edge?" asked Ron as he handed Claudia her skis.

"Devils Edge? Never, dude. I skied it a few years ago, but then it was stable. After a landslide a year and a half ago, parts of the slope collapsed, leaving a sharp edge. The remaining part is unstable. The smallest vibrations would cause an avalanche. We just avoid it."

Ron's eyebrows narrowed. "But I still see people skiing it."

"I don't know why they do. There's a big sign there that says danger, and the slope is way too steep."

"Hmm," said Ron as he watched Claudia finish getting ready. He snapped on his goggles. "Let's go!"

After about an hour and a half, they were done. Claudia went to see her students, and Ron went to look for his own instructor.

Claudia usually took a nap in her room during break time so she could recharge enough to power through the evening with Ron. As she went in through the lounge entrance, Paul the bartender, was on his way out.

Paul's face lit up like a Christmas tree. "Hey, stranger. I rarely see you in here. In fact, I was coming out to the snow to find you."

"Hi Paul." Claudia laughed. "It's gotten hectic." She

thought the coming out to see you was just a way of deflecting his own responsibility of not asking about her.

Paul exhaled with an exaggerated shoulder slump. "Tell me about it."

Claudia's eyebrows narrowed. "Have you seen Max around?" She wanted to add he hadn't been replying to my messages but decided not to.

"In fact," said Paul, "I was indeed coming to find you." He unzipped his right coat pocket and handed Claudia an envelope.

Claudia looked at the envelope and then at Paul, her chest tightening. "Is he okay? What's in it?"

"He's okay, to your first question. To the second, I don't know what's in it, but it's addressed to you. I guess you'll find out as soon as you open it." Paul tapped Claudia on the shoulder. "Good thing I saw you out here. It saved me time." He exhaled. "Please, come in later for some of Paul's special coffee." He turned and headed to the lounge.

Max wrote a letter. Why in the world would he not take her calls but write her a letter?

Claudia walked briskly to her room. She went in and locked the door behind her. Hands shaking, she ripped open the letter, her heart hammering in her chest.

31

WYATT

ALL AROUND HIM, PEOPLE WERE IN THE CHRISTMAS HOLIDAY mood, and it was terrific. They were skiing, snowboarding, tubing, skating, or just taking walks with a thermos of something hot.

Something always smelled good in the air. It could be from the lounge or blown by the wind from the German Market, a major attraction not far away. Wyatt sometimes played a game with himself to guess the food that was in the air. Sometimes it smelled like steak or baked goods, and other times just wood smoke.

Since he'd been in the resort twice, he'd run into people he knew from his job at New York City's stock exchange. They thought he was on vacation too. His was a working vacation, but it had gotten busier in the past few days.

Initially, the job was a piece of cake. But as the holiday got into full swing, and people started taking vacations and heading to Mountain Peak, their customer pool had gotten larger and larger. The reason for taking the job in the first place was to practice skiing, and so far, he'd gotten enough practice to last him a lifetime.

Wyatt was trying to live a better life, moving away from his playboy days. Claudia had blown his mind. It was usually him that abandoned the women, but this time around, Claudia wasn't easy to pin down. He'd made the fatal error of thinking she was in the bag already and focused on Riley when she threw herself at him.

The closer he got to Riley, the more obvious it became to him that she wasn't there for him. She was there for herself—to learn how to ski. In fact, it seemed she was the type of woman that liked being the center of attention. Leading you on, expressing enough interest to have you on a leash.

While he was transfixed by Riley, he'd neglected Claudia, and now he had a better understanding of the quote, a bird in the hand is worth two in the bush. For him, his bird in hand had flown, and the presence of Cameron Dawn wasn't helping matters in retrieving it.

This morning after practicing with Riley, she'd left him for a snowboarding class, and he had a little time on his hands. He decided to go find Claudia and invite her to come to the dance with him. He couldn't believe how he had abandoned her at the last dance once Riley appeared.

He headed for the lounge, smiling and nodding at some young women that dissolved in giggles as he passed. They were distractions. *Keep your eyes on the prize.* He wanted Claudia, and he believed she had a fondness for him too. But she was spending too much time with Ron. He hoped he wasn't too late again.

Wyatt wondered if Ron was trying to get back at him for

the event at their college dorm room many years ago. It wasn't his fault. Any man with blood flowing through his veins would have done precisely what he did.

He entered the building and walked to the lounge door. Wyatt pulled it open and stepped in and looked around. There was no sign of Claudia or Ron. He decided to take a seat and wait for a few minutes.

He was sure they would show up. They always met in the afternoon before disappearing for the rest of the day and night.

Wyatt ordered a mug of coffee and sat on one of the couches. He picked up a skiing magazine on the coffee table and flipped through. Each time the door opened, he would look up, then go back to the magazine.

Wyatt's mind drifted to many years ago in college when he'd shared a room with Ron. It was a weekend, and Ron had a family emergency and left for home. Wyatt was in the room, bored. Just like now, he'd been reading a magazine when Ron's girlfriend came to their dorm room looking for him.

Wyatt was a champion, well known on campus, and it was only natural that Ron's girlfriend was infatuated with him. He moved on her, and before he knew it, she gave him a blow job, then he fucked her. Wyatt felt terrible afterward, but she could have said no. A few weeks later, Ron and the girl broke up and changed rooms. Later Wyatt learned the girl had told Ron about the tryst.

Just then, the door to the lounge opened again and drew Wyatt away from his reminiscing. This time, Ron walked in. Wyatt expected Claudia to be behind him, but Ron's eyes darted around as if he was looking for someone. He spotted Wyatt, gave him a bro nod, then turned to leave.

Wyatt sprang to his feet. "Ron!"

Ron turned and raised his eyebrows as Wyatt approached. "Hi."

"I thought Claudia was with you. Have you seen her?"

Ron stood straight and looked at Wyatt. "Tired of Riley already? And now you're like yeah, I feel like Claudia now."

"Come on Ron, after all these years, you still haven't let sleeping dogs lie?"

"I have, but it's like déjà vu all over again. You can't find your own women. Only the ones I'm with seem to interest you."

"Dude, it's not my fault," said Wyatt. "After all these years, you haven't learned how to keep your women on a tight leash? They always gravitate toward me. Who is to blame here?"

A few people turned to look at them, then went back to what they were doing.

Ron opened his hands like a professor asking a rhetorical question. "Let's take a different approach, Webb. Are you a man without scruples?"

Blood rushed to Wyatt's head. The back of his neck crinkled with heat. That was his weakness. People had called him Judas, the selfish one, and here was Ron reiterating it. He had to get back at him. "You're always blaming other people for your inadequacies. Is it that the knife is not sharp, or the wielder doesn't know how to use it?"

Ron's nostrils flared. His jaw muscles clenched and unclenched.

Wyatt knew it was dangerous to corner a man, even a timid one. When you give them no means of escape, they have no choice but to go through you. Wyatt's heart dropped into his stomach when Ron moved his six feet two frame a step closer to him.

"You don't care for any other person," said Ron in a tight

voice. "It's always about you, you selfish motherfucker. Because you can doesn't mean you should. When you do, it's called taking advantage of of...exploiting. One day you'll be paid back in your own coins." Ron turned and walked away.

32

Claudia

CLAUDIA'S HANDS SHOOK SO MUCH SHE COULDN'T READ THE words. She took a deep breath and exhaled. Her hands steadied a little.

CLAUDIA, I GOT ALL YOUR CALLS AND TEXT MESSAGES, AND thank you so much for sending them. I'm sorry for not replying. I've always loved you, and in the past few days, I'd gotten to know you better, you are beautiful inside and out, with a beautiful soul.

I believe you care for me too, as I care for you. I dare say, I love you. I love you Claudia, and always have. People don't hurt who they love. I've been struggling with some challenges of my own, which I think would be wrong to expose you to. The best thing for me is to go away.

I took a position as a contractor with the agency and will

*be leaving as soon as possible. It's the best way. Love
you, Max.*

CLAUDIA WHIMPERED WHEN SHE FINISHED. "NO! NO!" MAX
had said he loved her. Tears streamed down her face. She
loved him too. He didn't have to run away from her. Whatever secret he was trying to hide, they could work it out
together. She had her own secrets too. Now history was about
to repeat itself. Now she was pushing someone else she loved
to do something they didn't want to do. Claudia believed
deep in her heart that once he left, he wouldn't come back
alive.

She had to stop him.

No matter what it took.

Claudia called his number; it rang and went to voicemail.
She called it a second time, and it went straight to voicemail.
He was avoiding her. He must still be in Mountain Peak.

She didn't know how, but seconds later, she was in her car
heading towards Max's place. She knew he would be gone,
but she kept on going.

Somehow through her blurry vision, she was able to drive
from the ski resort through Main Street's pedestrian and
vehicular traffic in one piece and was now ascending the hill
to Max's place. Now she was thinking more clearly.

Her heart leaped with joy when she drove into his
driveway and saw his truck still there with the back passenger
door open. Claudia parked behind it, got out of the car, and
rushed into the house through the slightly open front door.

Max came out from the passageway in his one-story
building carrying two suitcases. He saw Claudia, and his jaw
dropped. "Claudia." His voice was almost a whisper.
"What…what're you doing here?"

"I got your note. You can't leave," blurted Claudia.

Max gently put down the suitcases. He walked to the door, shut it, then took Claudia's hand. "Come."

Like a child on their first day of school, Claudia followed him and blurted, "Max...you can't leave."

Max picked up a remote control from the table, pushed a button, and the fireplace came on with a *whoosh*.

"Please listen to me, Max. I didn't mean to push you away, nor lose you. I don't know what secrets you have, but I have my own too. I killed our mother. I made her drive out to go buy me a unicorn candle, and she never came back."

Max's eyes widened. "What?"

"I killed our mother. I made her leave. I'm so sorry. I love you...and I don't want to lose you too."

Max squeezed her hand. "No, no, Claudia. What happened to your mother was an accident. You can't blame yourself. It-"

"No, Max. I made her go. If I hadn't insisted, she would've been home eating cake with us when the semi went through the intersection. Now I'm making you do something you don't want to do."

"Doctors can help."

Claudia exhaled. "It's my punishment to bear."

Max inhaled and exhaled. "Sit down, baby."

Claudia sat down. He'd called her baby; fresh tears streamed down her face.

Max walked over to the mini bar, poured two glasses of a straw-colored liquid, and walked back to Claudia. He sat down beside her.

"Cheers," said Max. He clicked his glass against Claudia's and tossed the drink down his throat.

Claudia held her drink, her hands shaking. She raised it to her lips. The aroma of caramel and vanilla hit her nostrils-bourbon. She emptied it as Max had done. The liquid scorched her mouth and burned all the way down to her stomach. The smell and taste were one and the same, leaving her with a warm fuzzy feeling in her girly bits.

Max took her glass, placed it on the table, then took her hands in his. "Claudia, I've always loved you since I saw you as Nicole's younger sister. Now that you're a woman, I love you even more. I'll get straight to the point. Right now, there's nothing else I would enjoy most than to spend the rest of my life with you. You've seen the scars on my body from my time in the Middle East. I'm damaged. It also left some scars on my mind. I was hurt and left for dead after a roadside bomb blew up our Bradly. I was thrown out of the car. As I struggled to get to my feet, another Marine that survived got out of the smoldering truck. He was on fire, his stomach ripped open, guts hanging out. The insurgents shot him. He collapsed onto another IED, and the blast threw me into a ditch." Max stopped talking and took a deep breath. "That second blast saved me. That was where the rescue team found me. That was all I remembered until days later when I woke up at the field hospital."

Claudia whimpered. "Oh my God."

Max squeezed her hand. "I was discharged from the army because of my injuries." He shook his head. "I couldn't stay away. It was all I knew. I was rehired as a contractor." Max's breathing got louder and faster. "The last girlfriend I had told me I have nightmares and talk in my sleep, but I didn't believe her. I woke up one night with my hand wrapped around her throat."

Claudia placed her hand on top of his and rubbed it back and forth.

"I knew about PTSD, but I didn't believe it could happen

to me. I'm anxious and have heightened reactions. It's only a matter of time before I hurt someone. And it could be you."

"Don't you see, Max? We...we're both damaged," said Claudia. "We're meant for each other."

Max threw his head back and exhaled.

"Please Max. Together, we will become stronger. In the past few weeks, talking about my birthday and my mother's death has helped, but it still lingers. We can support each other and get treated together." Claudia gazed into his eyes. "Please stay if you really love me." Claudia knew she was being manipulative, but people do that every day at different levels. You want something, and you're ready to give up something else in exchange for it. Maybe Ron's coaching was rubbing off too much on her. "Please don't go."

Max lowered his head and made eye contact with her. He exhaled. "Women."

She placed her hand on his fly and squeezed him. His cock went from soft to steel within seconds. "Fuck me, please."

Max got up and helped her out of her jacket.

"Wow!" laughed Claudia as Max lifted her in a fireman carry, the tense conversation seconds ago dissolved into play.

"Watch your head," said Max as he slowed down to pass through the door. "Welcome to *the bachelor pad*!" A dim, motion sensor light came on, illuminating Max's bedroom.

Claudia saw the king-size bed with black satin sheets moments before she was tossed onto it. She landed with a soft thud, and giggles exploded from her.

Max took off his clothes and shoes apart from his boxers. Claudia raised her head and looked at his body. His cock, like a thick plantain inserted in his underwear, strained the fabric of his boxers.

Max peeled off Claudia's socks, her pants, and underwear, and massaged the bottom of her feet one after the other.

A deep satisfied groan escaped Claudia's throat. After being on her feet all day skiing and skating, the release of tension brought about by Max's massage felt like the climax before the climax.

"What do you like?" asked Max, moving up and massaging her calf and inner thighs, causing her legs to quiver as if under some form of electrical stimulation.

"I like having you inside me." And she was ready. Her core was wet and slick, ready for him to slide in. The massage had been foreplay.

Max dipped a finger halfway into her and raised his finger. "Wow. You're more than ready." He gave her inner thigh one long suck, then scooted up and lay beside her so they faced each other. Their lips rubbed, teasing each other's, and then they kissed frantically.

Claudia moaned. Her body thrashed from side to side. She wanted him right now and traced her hand over his hard abdomen and slipped it into his boxers. The feel of his hard, pulsating member pulled words out of her. "It's so hard." She peeled his boxers off.

Max rolled on top of her, and Claudia spread her thighs to receive him. She ran her hand over his muscled back as he drove into her, taking her to new heights. Her breasts bobbed up and down with each thrust. He'd started slowly, but picked up the pace quickly. He pushed in and out, chasing his pleasure and giving at the same time.

Claudia rolled her hands over his muscled back, grabbing his ass cheeks and squeezing. Her fingers dug into his skin, urging him on.

"Fuck, Claudia."

Like the last time, Claudia watched his face, and she saw

and felt the signs of his impending climax. His nostrils flared, his muscles got tighter, and he fucked her faster and deeper. His breath came in gasps. That look alone pushed all kinds of pleasure buttons inside her, and Claudia's orgasm took her by surprise.

Moments later, Max's body tightened. Claudia crossed her legs over his butt, pulling him in and keeping him there. He moaned and groaned, then emptied inside her.

Claudia felt Max's weight on her driving the breath out of her, then he rested on his elbow, giving her room to breathe. They stayed in that position as they caught their breath.

"You've got me, Claudia Kraner. One can love from afar, but this"—he kissed her nipple—"you have to be present for."

Claudia felt so good inside, and sleepy too. Probably a combination of the bourbon, terrific sex, and Max's warm body close to hers. Her eyes soon shut in sleep.

Claudia's eyes flew open. Where was she? She heard snoring beside her and saw Max. It all came rushing back. She'd come to stop Max from leaving. And it looked like she'd succeeded. Then she heard her alarm again. That's what woke her up.

Claudia leaned over the bed and grabbed her jacket. She unzipped a pocket, retrieved her phone, and turned off her alarm. She'd always set her alarm so she wouldn't oversleep to meet Ron.

"Ron," whispered Claudia under her breath. This was the last day of training. She mustn't let him down. Pulse racing, she jumped off the bed and groped around the floor, looking for her panties.

33

Ron left the lounge as fast as he could. His heart pounded in his chest as if he'd just finished an ice-skating sprint race. He'd almost punched Wyatt in the face. That would have been disastrous for him because Wyatt would have bled all over the place, and then pressed charges when the cops arrived.

Ron got to his room, the fastest he'd ever walked from the lounge. Once inside, he paced back and forth, thinking about the day his girlfriend in college told him she'd slept with Wyatt. At first, he'd thought she was joking, but soon realized it was out of character. She wasn't a slut and had been burdened by guilt and shame. He really loved that girl, and that asshole fucked her because he could. *Calm down, Ron. A lot of water has passed under that bridge.*

He took a few deep breaths and exhaled through his mouth to calm himself. Whoever coined the phrase *nice guys finish last* knew what they were talking about. Wyatt, the jerk of all jerks, already had Claudia under his belt, and she was going nuts trying to win him back. And Riley, whom he hoped this photoshoot/vacation thing would be his opportunity to get to know her better, got hijacked by Wyatt Webb as well.

This was becoming a disaster. If Riley was not on the phone with her agent, she was with Wyatt. He might as well remove her photos as screensaver on his phone and computer.

Ron shook his head and quoted Scripture. "To those who have, more shall be given unto them." It wasn't fair.

Maybe he was on the wrong side of history. Those that do wrong seem to get the upper hand and are even celebrated. Worst case scenario they get a slap on the wrist. But people like him who try to do the right thing get the short end of the stick.

Ron would bet his left testicle that Wyatt had slept with Claudia. But he didn't understand why Wyatt still hovered around her while focusing on Riley. Maybe he had a soft spot for Claudia.

Ron chuckled. "Wyatt in love?" Wonders would never end. But who wouldn't like Claudia? Once you spent time with her, you'd fall in love with her.

He knew there was chemistry between him and Claudia. A friendship had developed between them. Maybe he should make a move and sleep with her, just to spite Wyatt.

Ron laughed out loud. *You're losing your mind,* he said to himself. What if he made a move and she said no? That would really make him the biggest loser. He pushed that thought away. He and Claudia had worked their plan hard. She had trained him, and he was confident he would impress Riley with his skiing. He was sure Claudia's makeover would impress Wyatt, and he would bite. Once a dog, always a dog.

Ron finally calmed down. Today was their last day of

dancing, and he had a few surprises up his sleeve. He pulled out his cell phone and made two calls.

34

Claudia

"You have a date with Ron?" asked Max in a sleepy voice after he opened his eyes and asked her why she was dressing up in a hurry.

"Yes! No. It's ballroom dancing."

"Dancing? What...what about it?" Max was half asleep, his question guarded.

"I'm taking ballroom dancing, and Ron's my partner. I set the alarm to remind me."

"Thank God," muttered Max. "I thought you wanted me to take you. You've worn me out. I'll see you at the resort tomorrow, okay?" Max pulled the covers over his head.

Back in her car, Claudia raced down the hill with a satisfied smile on her face. Max was staying.

The more she thought about the dancing ahead, the more she knew she was not in a state to dance up close with anyone. She'd been skiing before coming to visit Max. Her panties-well, she needed a shower and change of clothes before dancing.

Instead of taking the road that led out of town, Claudia changed direction. She headed toward the lodge for a shower and a change of clothes. She sent a voice text to Ron that she might be a few minutes late and prayed she wouldn't come across anyone to slow her down at the lodge.

There were people on the corridor when she arrived, but she made it to her room without meeting Wyatt in particular. Claudia was in and out of the shower in no time. She tossed her dirty clothes in the almost full laundry hamper, put on fresh underwear, and went to her closet for jeans and a blouse.

Claudia cried out loud, "No, no." The red dress she'd worn to the dance was the only clean thing hanging in her closet. She checked the time on her phone, then looked at the hamper. All her clothes were hiding in plain sight. She had about ten minutes before it would be a hit or miss to get to the dance on time.

She could wear her red dress, but she needed to do laundry too. Maybe when she got back? Claudia heaved a sigh of relief when she found a pair of stockings in her suit-case. The red dress it was then. Her legs and other places would feel cold. She would load the washing machine now, then later tonight put the clothes in the dryer.

A whiff of stale sweat assaulted her nostrils as she hurried off with her hamper to the laundry down the hall from her room. She loaded the washing machine, turned it on, and rushed back to her room to freshen her face and take off.

With her down jacket zipped up to cover her neck and her outfit and keep her warm, Claudia left her room and locked her door behind her. As she hurried toward the exit to the lodge, she looked at her phone. Now, she was late. A call to

Ron now would be appropriate. She would call while driving to the-

"Claudia?"

Claudia stiffened but continued walking. *Jesus, who is it now?*

"Claudia!"

She couldn't help herself and whirled around. It was Ron. "Ron!" Claudia suddenly felt light and giddy. She smiled. "I was just about to call you."

Ron jogged up to her, all smiles. "I was running late too. Good thing we came out almost at the same time. This is the last day of training. Are you as excited as I am?"

Claudia hesitated. "Kind of. But at the same time, sad." Claudia would have preferred it to continue. She'd developed a fondness for Ron, like the boys she went fishing with as a kid. "Every good thing must come to an end, right?"

Together they exited the building.

"Since we're both here," said Ron, "and it's the last day, maybe we should ride in the same car."

Claudia was used to driving her car alone to the dance studio, but why not? "Your car or mine?"

"My car. Well, my rental. I'll drive."

After the initial chat of how their plan had been working out so far, they drove in companionable silence most of the way. Claudia's thoughts were more on how tomorrow would end. Would Wyatt be blown away when he saw her at the dance? Now she could dance and had a better sense of fashion, but there was nothing to see. Nothing had changed in terms of physical appearance. She should at least buy a new dress and get her hair done. Was she shallow? Basing it all on looks? Wyatt already liked her; it was her dancing that wasn't up to par. She shifted her thoughts to Ron.

Ron had become a good skier, and impressing Riley

wouldn't be a problem for him. She glanced at Ron, and he turned to meet her gaze.

Ron smiled. "What?"

"Nothing. It just hit home that this is our last day. It felt good to look forward to something." Claudia leaned closer and pecked him on the cheek. "Thank you for everything."

"It's a quid pro quo! You scratch my back, and I scratch yours." Ron's eyes darted between Claudia and the road. "You think I'd be taking you dancing if you weren't teaching me how to ski?"

Claudia laughed and punched him playfully on the shoulder.

"Ouch! Easy girl, never attack a guy with his hands on the wheel." He laughed out loud, then went quiet. "Thank you, Claudia, from the bottom of my heart."

Claudia looked out of the window to keep busy. They drove on in silence. This time, it was an uncomfortable silence. She saw the dance studio coming up and expected to hear the tick tick tick of the signal indicator, but Ron continued. She turned toward him. "You drove past the studio."

"We're done, remember?" said Ron with a laugh. "We have another appointment. Well, *you* have an appointment."

Five minutes later, he pulled into a strip mall and stopped in front of a hair salon. "You have a hair appointment. My treat."

Claudia's mouth was still hanging open when Ron strolled over to the passenger side and opened the door.

Speechless, Claudia followed him into the salon.

"Hello," said a blonde with an apron tied around her waist.

Claudia looked around. It was a hairdresser franchise - she'd been to one of their stores before. They all looked and smelled alike. The odor of heated plastic from the blow dryer, the smell of blow-dried hair, and the flowery scent of shampoo reached her nostrils. There were about eight stations in front of a long horizontal mirror. Seven of the seats were occupied by women getting their hair done. Some of the hair-dressers chatted with the women as they fussed over them.

A flat-screen TV showed people doing Christmas shop-ping, the volume drowned by the humming of blow dryers, the buzzing of hair clippers, and the *snap snap snap* of scissors.

"Welcome, how can we help you today?" asked the apron-wearing lady.

Ron smiled. "Hi, we're here for an appointment for Claudia?"

"Yes, please follow me."

Ron leaned close to Claudia.

She could smell the richness of his cologne. Was he coming to kiss her? Her pulse picked up a notch.

"Trust me," he said. "I know what's good for you."

Disappointed and confused, Claudia said, "Really?" She added an eye roll for good measure. But she nodded and followed the lady to a chair.

The hairdresser pointed at a coat rack against the wall. "You can hang your coat over there."

Claudia removed her coat and noticed Ron was just staring at her with an exploratory and suggestive gaze. She looked at herself and remembered she had a dress on instead of her regular drab outfit. Heat rushed to her cheeks. Was that desire in his eyes? She walked over to the rack and felt the heat from Ron's eyes on her ass.

Ron cleared his throat and waved his hand in the air as he spoke. "Give her a two-tone messy bob. You know, to give a disheveled texture appearance."

Disheveled? Claudia shot him a look.

Ron mouthed, *Trust me*, then said, "I'm just going to step out. I'll be back before you know it."

Claudia, still lost for words, watched him in the mirror as he walked out of the salon.

The hairdresser started to examine Claudia's hair. "Yeah," she said, nodding, "the two-tone bob will look great on you. Was that your boyfriend? He has a good eye for what will look good on you."

Claudia felt a longing in her heart. She wanted to say yes, but… "He's a photographer and a friend." Her voice trailed off.

"Aha. He has expertise."

Claudia only cut her hair when it started to get unruly. She watched in fascination as the hairdresser went to work. Claudia couldn't say for sure how long it took, probably under an hour, but she was transformed in that time.

Ron came back at that moment as if he'd been lurking outside the door. His face brightened, and a wistful smile parted his lips. "Nice!" He looked like he was admiring something he couldn't have.

The hairdresser walked over to the computer station and said the amount out loud.

"Remember, it's my treat," said Ron as he whipped out his wallet.

Claudia wanted to object but remembered the saying *Don't look a gift horse in the mouth.*

Back in the car, Ron started the engine. "One more stop, and we're done for the night."

"Where're we going?" asked Claudia in a bubbly voice. She loved going to new places.

"I'm hungry, and I'm sure you are too. We'll eat, then put all those dancing lessons to practice."

"Okay, but my treat. I won't come out of the car unless you agree."

Ron looked at Claudia with mock surprise. "Jesus, woman! You don't have to threaten me."

Claudia laughed. "I didn't know you were this funny. I'm not threatening you. I insist. By the way, how did you know this hairdo would look good on me?"

"That's easy, I've seen your face a million times in my mind's eye."

He was treating her like a girlfriend. Better than any boyfriend she'd ever had. Claudia felt something shift inside her. Like an awakening for Ron.

The place they stopped to eat was a restaurant where you could eat, drink, then hit the dance floor. Claudia and Ron did just that. Between the two of them, they drank a bottle of wine. Claudia drank a little bit more. She'd barely had anything all afternoon.

By the time they left two hours after they got there, Claudia knew she felt something for Ron that left a fluttery sensation in her chest and stomach.

It was almost midnight when they walked through the doors of the lounge. The boom of music drifted out to the passageway. Ron had cleaned out his car, and he carried a shopping bag with him as he walked her to her room.

Claudia stopped at her door. "Thank you so much. This was the most fun I've had in a long time." She remembered Bradford and Max. She'd been happy with them too, but this was different. Ron fulfilled a different set of needs.

"The pleasure is all mine. Your face is like an open book. It shows what you feel, and your reaction the whole evening made me feel good. Thank you."

Claudia bit her nails, then her lower lip. She wanted to

invite him in. Not for anything but just to hang around. But she knew he would say no. He was such a good guy. But the next thing Ron did gave her an opening.

Ron pushed the shopping bag to her. "Here, for you. Your outfit for tomorrow."

Claudia's eyes widened. "What?"

"I bought it while you were getting your hair done."

Claudia was already shaking her head. "No, I can't accept it. You've already done so much for me."

"I insist. It's my birthday gift to you." Ron smiled. "I promised I'd never miss your birthday, and I missed the last one, but I bought a gift."

"That's not logical. You're trying to cheat. You only found out after the fact. This year doesn't count."

"Okay, it's for your next birthday then."

"I'll only accept it on one condition."

"What?"

"You'll be the first to see me wearing it."

Ron rubbed his chin and appeared to be deep in thought. "Fine, I'll dress up early and take you to the dance."

"No, I mean tonight."

Ron cocked his head. "I…I don't think that's a good idea."

Claudia inhaled, then exhaled. She pursed her lips. "I'm sorry, you're probably right. It must be all that wine. I thought I danced it all off."

Ron cleared his throat. "Ummm…I should probably go… back to my room. Have a good night."

"You too, and thanks." Claudia removed her key from her pocket and reached for her door.

Ron turned and walked away.

Claudia tried to get the key in but couldn't. She had drunk more than a few.

"Are you okay?" asked Ron from a few feet away.

Claudia looked up and shook her head. "I…I can't get the key in." Her voice was shaky. "I should lay off the wine."

"Hold on, let me take a look." Ron jogged back toward her.

35

CAMERON

"OH, YOU DIDN'T HAVE TO COME BACK," SAID CLAUDIA. "I'll eventually sort it out. It's only a key and a hole. I'll eventually get it in."

Ron leaned closer to her. "Here, let me try." Her hair brushed against his face. He could smell her, the strong sweet flowery smell from the salon, with some vanilla. Their fingers touched as he took the key from her. It felt like a jolt of electricity had just passed through him.

The key slid in smoothly, and Ron turned it. It unlocked with a click. He turned to look at Claudia, and she was right there, inches from his face.

She pressed herself against him. "My knight in shining armor." This was the first time she'd ever come after a man like this. She rubbed her breast against him.

Before Ron could react, her lips were on his, nibbling and tugging. A sudden onslaught of heat spread from his crotch outward.

"Sorry, I lied."

Ron knew her invitation to see her new dress could be phrased as an invitation to see her in her birthday dress. What wasn't obvious to him was how he was going to respond. How to extricate himself from this without ruffling any feathers. He was the good guy. The guy who didn't take advantage of people.

Claudia raised her leg and nudged his crotch.

That fortitude he'd worn like a badge of honor clattered to the floor like a useless politician's button. Like a man possessed, Ron held her face and kissed her. His tongue probed her mouth. She tasted of wine and mint. They stumbled through the door and into her room, and he kicked the door shut with the heel of his shoes.

You can still stop this, Cameron Dawn. Just stop kissing her. Easier said than done. Ron's hands and fingers had minds of their own. They roamed over her body, squeezing and massaging. Her body was so soft and felt so good in his hands. His lips were still glued to hers, their tongues tangling and untangling. She tasted so sweet.

Claudia took Ron's hand and placed it underneath her dress on her inner thigh. The heat on his hands felt like a hot blanket on a cold winter night.

The skin of her thigh was soft and smooth. Ron squeezed and headed north. Soon his probing hands brushed up against the mound of her swollen pussy.

Claudia moaned and pulled her lips away with a smack.

Ron pulled at the edges of her panties, and a finger made its way into her core.

Claudia's breath caught, and she whimpered.

Ron's fears were confirmed. She was soaked and ready.

She held him tighter, and her hips started to move.

Ron tossed his jacket to the side, followed by his shirt and T-shirt.

Claudia raised her dress, and Ron helped, pulling it over her head, exposing her toned body. Ron watched like a deer caught in the headlight of a car as Claudia reached behind and unclipped her bra. Her boobs spilled into his hands.

A strangled groan escaped her throat as he rolled her nipple between his fingers, then introduced his lips to her erect nipples.

Ron felt her hands on his belt and pants.

Within seconds, her hands were on each side of his hips, and his boxers and pants came slid to his ankles.

"Claudia," said Ron, slightly breathless, voice tight. "You don't have to do this…because I bought you a dress."

Claudia was on her knees, looking up at him. "I'm going to fuck you because I want to."

Ron watched in amazement as his thick cock disappeared down her throat.

She held his cock by the base and bobbed her head up and down. His whole length slid in and out, massaged by her wet lips and tongue.

"Fuck." Ron's feet, planted solidly on the carpet, started to shake as wave after wave of pleasure crashed through him. He threw his head back, enjoying every moment.

Claudia got up, grabbed him by the cock, and led him toward the bed. Ron kicked off his shoes and followed. She put a finger on his chest and pushed him onto the bed.

Ron took in her succulent breasts, pointed nipples, and knew there was nothing he could do to stop where this was going.

"Now, fuck me." She straddled him, grabbed his cock, pushed aside her panties, and guided him in.

The sensation drew a gasp from both of them.

Claudia began slowly, then started to move her hips faster and faster.

Ron knew it would be a miracle if he lasted more than a minute. The pleasure was like having several fingers coated with sweet candy thrust into your mouth, while the chocolate bar you crave is dangled at arm's length. His eyes were on her face as she chased her pleasure, looking for the right angle or sweet spot for maximum pleasure.

Claudia was very expressive, making several different faces as she grasped, then lost the sweet spot.

Ron cupped her ass, squeezed, and hefted her up and down his cock.

"Yes, that feels good," moaned Claudia and moved her hips like a belly dancer, grinding into him, rubbing her clit against him.

Ron was breathing hard, fighting the wave of intense pleasure knocking on his door, threatening to grab him like an airport luggage conveyor belt for a straight ride to game over. He didn't want to come before her.

But Claudia was now riding him like the jockey The Fokker riding the Mountain Peak derby winner, Slippery Dick.

Ron fought to distract himself, but the look on her face made it impossible. Then he heard the sound of crickets somewhere in the corner of the room. It took Ron a moment to realize it was his cell phone, in the pocket of his pants, wherever he'd kicked them to.

"Don't even think of getting off this bed," said Claudia, slightly breathless.

"No, I won't." Ron knew who it was. Riley. Wanting to talk with him until sleep took her. Something he did to make himself indispensable to her. But now he had a bird in hand. Fuck the ones in the bush.

Claudia didn't break rhythm; she continued going at it. But for Ron, the distraction was manna from heaven. It got him off that darn conveyor belt and bought him a few minutes.

He had her on her back, pounding into her with renewed vigor. Then on her hands and knees, taking her from behind. The visual was amazing. The curves of her butt now became the new screen saver in his mind. Then she was on top again, and this time they got on the conveyor belt together, moaning and groaning as they climaxed together.

They lay on their backs on the bed, trying to catch their breaths. Everything was great until Ron realized he was no different from Wyatt. But she had invited him in for something.

"Oh my God," muttered Claudia. "You made me come so hard."

"Are you still going to try on the dress?"

"That's for tomorrow. You came to help me with the door, remember?"

"The key couldn't fit in, yeah, right?"

Claudia giggled. "Well, you fell for it."

They both laughed, and soon Claudia nudged his cock with her knee, and they were off to the races again.

By the time Ron snuck out of her room two hours later with Claudia sleeping peacefully under the sheets, he was convinced she was what he needed in his life.

36

Claudia

CLAUDIA DRIFTED AWAKE. DID A SOUND WAKE HER UP? THEN she heard it again. It was the blare of her phone alarm, reminding her it was time to get up and get ready to practice with Ron. For some unknown reason, she felt so good—*why?* Then she smelled the fragrance from her freshly done hair. There was also another smell—the smell of Ron's cologne all around her and the smell of sex. The events of last night rushed back to her mind, and she smiled.

Claudia brought her hands out from underneath the sheet and spread them out sideways. She felt the smooth cold fabric of the bedsheet, but no warm body. Her eyes flew open. "Ron?"

Her eyes got used to the dimness of the room, and she confirmed what she already knew. Ron's clothes were missing—he'd left. She'd tricked him and fucked him. Claudia remembered the trick, and a smile danced on her lips.

Then it quickly faded. What was she doing? In the course of two weeks, she'd slept with three men. She was a slut.

She would have to talk to Riley and apologize to her. Then there was Wyatt. But she was not in a relationship with Wyatt, and Ron was not in a relationship with Riley either. No harm, no foul.

Claudia let out a deep breath and felt a little better. She didn't owe anyone an apology. Unethical, yes. A tramp, no.

Claudia sat on her bed naked, hugging her knees, with the sheet draped over her shoulder. Her newfound relief suddenly evaporated. She was missing something. It was at the tip of her brain, as someone would say a name was at the tip of their tongue.

"Max!"

She had to find a way to figure this out, rationalize it. Men do it all the time—they sow wild oats. Are women allowed to do the same? This was the twenty-first century, not the Middle Ages. Claudia sighed and hugged her knees tighter. How did she get here?

The snooze of her alarm kicked in, and Claudia had to make a move, get ready for the day. Then she groaned. All her clothes were in the laundry. It was still dark out, so she contemplated making a naked dash down the hall to the laundry and put on some of her clean clothes while there. Then she remembered they hadn't been dried. The thought of wearing something cold made her break out in goosebumps.

Claudia looked around and saw her red dress crumpled on the floor. That would do. She put it on, grabbed her room key and phone, and headed for the laundry.

Her clothes were still there. She loaded them in the dryer and went back to her room. She'd be back in an hour. Back in her room, she brushed her teeth, showered, and put on the red dress again. It was almost an hour, so she went back to the laundry.

The dryer was still going, but the clothes were dry. Claudia stuffed them into her laundry bag, taking a few seconds break now and then because some of her clothes were damn hot when the door opened. Claudia swung around. It was Jane. "Jane!"

"Claudia! You're all dressed up. What...where are you going?"

Claudia groaned. "Nowhere. You know how it is. We've been so busy all my clothes were dirty. This was the only available thing."

Jane walked toward the washer. "Tell me about it." She put her black hair in a ponytail and held it with a scrunchie. Then she started to load her clothes in the washer.

"How was your trip? We haven't talked since you came back."

"It was fun—a lot of sex. New Hampshire was awesome. We went on the Polar Express, The Conway Railroad. It's an old-fashioned train ride. Like traveling in the past with some amazing scenery."

"Wow, nice," said Claudia.

"Talking of sex, you're glowing." Jane's eyebrows narrowed. "What's going on? Before we left, you were humping Wyatt. Now I see him all over Riley. And Cameron is hanging with you." Jane's eyes widened. "Oh my God!" She raised her palms to her mouth. "You guys swapped? Open relationship?"

"No, get your mind out of the gutter." But she was close. *You know, in the past couple of weeks, I slept with all three guys.* But she didn't say that. Instead, she said, "Ron and Riley are trying to impress each other and have been training secretly to improve their skiing skills. Wyatt was already assigned to Riley, but Ron asked me to help him."

Jane nodded. "Okay. If you say so. Are you coming to the party tomorrow?" Jane looked at Claudia's head. "That's what it is. I knew something looked different. You did your hair. That style looks so good on you."

Claudia wanted to share with her friend that it was Ron's idea but decided not to. "Just something different."

"Anyway, I have to run. I'll be at the party tonight. We'll catch up some more then."

Back in her room, Claudia remembered she didn't have to leave early again since training with Ron was over. Her first class started at 9:00 am. She would just wait until then. She noticed the bag with the outfit Ron had bought leaning against the wall and was amazed she'd forgotten all about it last night. A smile tugged the corner of her lips. The heat last night was off the charts.

She tried it on, and it was a perfect fit.

37

Claudia

WHEN YOU'RE USED TO A ROUTINE AND IT ENDS, YOU NEED to fill the void with something else, otherwise you'll be bored out of your mind. Luckily for Claudia, this morning her schedule took her to the pond she and Max had cleaned off not too long ago. She just wanted to avoid Wyatt, Riley, Ron, and Max for now. She would be embarrassed to look Ron in the face because of last night. Wyatt, she wanted to surprise later.

The skating class went without incident, and when she was done, she headed straight for her room. There was a lot on her mind.

It was then it struck Claudia she'd slept with two different men just hours apart. She'd dug herself a deep hole. *Claudia, what are you doing?* Ron was what an ideal boyfriend should be in her mind. She'd always loved Max, and now she'd made him stay back. She owed him. Then there was Wyatt. What was Wyatt to her?

As Claudia stepped into the lounge, Max was coming out, and his face lit up like Time Square at midnight on New Year's Day. He had a big smile, like a kid who has just gotten the present he really wanted from Santa.

"Hey, how are you?" Max's smile wavered. "You look frazzled. Everything okay?"

"I'm all right, just a little tired." She was tired all right, but that wasn't the reason. Claudia was worried, not sure what she was doing. She'd just stopped him from doing what he felt was right for himself. But could she become whom he wanted her to become? Claudia took a deep breath and forced a smile.

Max's forehead furrowed. "Did you say you were going dancing last night? Because I had nightmares about dancing all night." Max's smile was back.

Claudia laughed and nodded. "So I guess you're not coming tonight for the dance."

"Count me out. I have a busy day and should be fatigued by nightfall."

Good, thought Claudia.

"Plus, I'll have to call the agency and let them know I'm still thinking about the offer."

Claudia's heart stopped. She thought he'd already made up his mind. "Thinking about it? I thought your mind was made up." She cautioned herself to stop making her hole deeper. She was already deep enough. He was doing all this because of her. What if he found out about Ron?

"Are you sure you're okay? Maybe you should go take a nap."

"I will. So which agency are you talking about?"

"The CIA. You never want to slam the door on anyone or burn bridges. They'll take it as I changed my mind but am open for discussion in the future."

"The CIA. Is the job dangerous?"

Max laughed. "Is skiing dangerous?"

"Could be," said Claudia with a non-committal shrug. "If you run into a tree or fly off a mountain top."

"I agree with you," said Max. "Anyway, I have to go. I'll see you tomorrow morning. Now go get that nap." He leaned in and kissed her on the cheek.

Claudia watched him go, whistling, walking with a spring to his step. She'd never seen him so happy. Max had always had a special place in her heart, and she wanted it to remain that way.

Claudia got back to her room, changed, and literally crawled into bed. By the time her alarm went off several hours later as a reminder to get ready for the dance, she was refreshed. She hurried off to the bathroom to shower, then changed after that. Her focus was now on Wyatt and her preparation for the dance. Would it succeed? Concerns about Max drifted to the back burner.

38

Claudia

CLAUDIA WAS ALL DRESSED UP AND APPLYING RED LIPSTICK when there was a knock on her door. She knew it must be Ron coming to see her in the dress as he'd promised and take her to the dance.

The black dress with a halter neck and side slit, was just beautiful. The slit showed off Claudia's toned legs up to mid-thigh. It was tight and hugged her figure like a second skin.

Claudia looked over her shoulder at the full-length mirror on the closet door. The fabric grabbed her butt and showed the lines of her panties; she didn't like that. Claudia remembered the black thong in her suitcase and recalled seeing it when she'd taken out the red dress. She went looking for it, praying she hadn't thrown it away.

Luckily, the thong was still there. Quickly, Claudia changed into it, and when she looked in the mirror, the fabric over her butt looked smooth, with no lines.

As she looked at her complete ensemble, she wondered if

Wyatt would approve. For the life of her, Claudia couldn't say exactly why it was so important to her that she impress him. He'd continued to focus on Riley while claiming he was trying to extricate himself. Anyway, tonight was the litmus test. Getting Wyatt's full attention would prove to herself that she had what it took to appeal to men. *Was that it?* She wanted validation. Two more rapid knocks on her door brought her back to the present.

Claudia spoke over her shoulder. "One second!" She checked herself in the mirror one more time, put on her heels, and headed for the door. She knew she looked good. If she were a guy, she would go after herself. Claudia pulled the door all the way open in a sweeping arch, as if presenting an award on stage.

Ron stood there in a black suit, white shirt, and a bow tie. His mouth dropped open, then closed again like a pelican swallowing a fish. *Pelican?* Finally, he found his voice. "It's even more beautiful than I imagined."

"You really have an eye for fashion, Ron. I love the outfit!" Claudia took a step back and looked him over. "You look great too! Come in, I'm almost done." She walked to the bed to get her purse and phone, aware of Ron's eyes on her. Heat rushed through her body. From the way Ron looked at her, you would never guess he'd ever seen her naked before, nor made love to her. "I'm ready."

They walked side by side to the lounge. The music was like a magnet drawing them closer and closer.

"I'll let you make an entrance," said Ron. "I wish I could stop the music and make an announcement."

Claudia punched him playfully on the shoulder.

"I'll open the door, and you walk in." Ron paused. "You look HOT. Go get him!"

Claudia's nostrils flared. "Thanks." Her heartbeat

matched the thumping of the music.

Ron opened the door, and she stepped in.

Flashing strobe lights and loud music enveloped her. Claudia surveyed the room. She knew she had indeed made an entrance. People stopped in mid-conversation to stare, then continued with their conversations. Not seeing Wyatt, she headed for the bar. She was surprised Paul was not there. Instead, a young woman was working. As she was about to order a drink, someone yelled out her name above the loud music. Claudia turned. Wyatt stood there with Riley, his eyes almost popping out of his head.

"My God! You are beautiful!" said Wyatt in a halting voice. "I love your hair. So, what can I get you?" He looked around, all giddy. "Wait, I know." He turned to the bartender. "A daiquiri for the stunning lady, and a Manhattan for me."

Claudia smiled and finally spoke. "Hi, Wyatt. Riley."

Riley, her lips drawn into a thin line, nodded at Claudia.

Claudia was waiting for Wyatt to order Riley's drink before speaking so she wouldn't interrupt him. But he just stood there, smiling sheepishly, his full focus on Claudia.

Riley flipped her hair out of her face. "Hey Wyatt, what about that dance?"

Eyes still on Claudia, Wyatt said, "The next dance is with Claudia."

There was an awkward moment as Riley stared in disbelief.

Ron seemed to appear from nowhere. "Hey, guys. Riley! I've been looking all over for you."

Riley looked dazed. "Huh?"

Ron led her by the arm. "Come on."

Claudia was glad Ron had come to the rescue. Their drinks came as soon as were poured.

"Cheers." They clinked glasses and raised the drinks to

their lips.

Claudia was parched. She drained her glass and felt it travel down to her stomach. A cozy warm feeling started from there and spread out, engulfing her body. With an empty stomach, the buzz was instant. "Wow," she muttered. "That feels good."

Wyatt watching her, laughed. "This reminds me of that night at Hawks Lair." He emptied his glass in one gulp and asked the bartender for seconds for both.

"That's right. You made my birthday a day to remember."

Wyatt wound his hand around Claudia's waist. "Can I dance with you for the rest of the night?"

"I haven't even agreed to one dance," said Claudia. "And you're no longer avoiding me?"

"I wasn't avoiding you. Not at all. Riley was just too demanding. I think you were avoiding me. Every evening, you just disappeared."

Claudia knew it was when she and Ron had been working their plan. "I'm here now." Their second drinks arrived, and Claudia took a sip of hers.

"Claudia, I don't know what it is about you, but you've occupied my whole mind. You've stolen my heart."

Claudia beamed. What Wyatt said was like music to her ears. "What about that dance?" She also liked the new music that had just started to play.

"Sure." Wyatt tossed his second drink down, Claudia did the same, and they hit the dance floor.

Wyatt spoke up within a minute of dancing. "I can see you've acquired some new skills."

Claudia smiled, enjoying every minute of it. Now she was in control of her steps, moving in sync to the beat. When the music changed to a slow one, she let Wyatt take her hand and pull her closer. It was electric.

After every few pop dance songs, the DJ would throw in a Christmas song, a reminder of the season. Claudia and Wyatt sat in a corner and ordered new drinks, singing aloud and saying sweet nothings.

By the time a slow number came back on, the alcohol had infused into her body. She dragged Wyatt to the dance floor, her body engulfed with the heat. The strobe lights criss-crossing the room made it appear like she was being consumed by fire.

Wyatt pressed his hard cock against her, and his hands left burning smudges as they traveled up and down her body.

Claudia wanted to prolong the *want* as much as possible, but she just couldn't take it anymore. Her core was sleek, wet, and ready. She nibbled Wyatt's ear lobe and whispered, "Let's take this to my room."

Wyatt didn't need to be told twice. Still holding her hand, he pulled her off the dance floor.

Outside the lounge, Wyatt pinned Claudia against the wall of the hallway. Claudia's heartbeat and the thumping of music resonated as one through her body. Her tongue drove into his mouth as her knee nudged his cock to the left and then right.

Fuck. An animal-like groan escaped Wyatt's throat. "Let's go." His voice was so tight, Claudia just barely heard him.

At her door, Claudia fumbled for a moment. This was not a repeat of last night. She was saturated with alcohol, and her dexterity was the victim.

Finally, she grasped the key and drove it into the hole. Claudia opened the door and tried to pull the key out, but Wyatt was already urging her into the room, his breath hot against her neck. His cock, pressed against her butt, felt like a hot branding rod. Her fingers slid off the door key, and they stumbled in.

Wyatt kicked the door shut.

39

CAMERON

AS RON ENTERED THE LOUNGE, HE SAW A COUPLE GET UP from their table and head for the dance floor, taking their personal effects with them.

Ron headed to the table and took it over. From that vantage point, he could see Riley, dressed in a red body-hugging evening gown holding a red clutch, her blond hair fanning out behind her like flames.

Wyatt, the bastard, wore a black suit. Ron begrudgingly acknowledged that he looked good, then his eyes moved on to Claudia. His breath caught-she was so beautiful. He still couldn't believe he'd slept with her. It was totally out of character for him, but damn, he would do it again. Maybe he was changing.

He thought of his girlfriend many years ago. Was she caught up with the euphoria of Wyatt being a champion? It was a tough decision. He decided that the best approach was to avoid situations where you could get tempted or lose control. Things like visiting a movie producer or any powerful person in their hotel room for a meeting instead of the office should be a no-no.

There is always someone in the office or in the building. In a hotel room, it's just you and the person. If they make an indecent proposal to you that could advance your career, it would be a challenge to say no. And if they drop a date rape drug in your drink, and you're in their hotel room, they'll have you open like 7-11. Life was just complicated. Just don't put yourself in a situation where your sense of judgment could be compromised.

Ron smiled at Wyatt's reaction to Claudia. He seemed to have been bewitched and quickly abandoned Riley as if she was contagious. As he looked at Riley, the music and the strobe lights flashing back and forth appeared to create an ominous background against her.

Wyatt ordered drinks, and things started to deteriorate for Riley. Even when Riley seemed to be talking to Wyatt, he didn't look her way, but his lips were moving. He was one hundred percent focused on Claudia. Ron wasn't sure, but to him, it looked like Riley was about to melt down. He decided to make a move. He placed his jacket over his chair and hurried off to the bar to rescue Riley, hoping no one would steal his seat the same way he'd stolen it.

"Hey, guys. Riley! I've been looking all over for you."

Riley looked dazed. "Huh?"

Ron led her by the arm. "Come on." He was glad Riley followed without any objection. As they approached the table, a couple hovered around the table as if trying to decide if they should take it or not. "Sorry, guys, that's our table."

"Oh," said the man, and they moved on.

"It's been a long time since we sat down together," said Ron. "You've really been working hard at skiing."

Riley gazed at him as if he was speaking a foreign language. She blinked, then folded her hands over her stomach. "So…sorry, what was that?"

Ron repeated himself.

"Yes! That's true," said Riley, suddenly enthusiastic. She glanced at the bar, then back to Ron. "You've been busy too. I barely see you."

"Mmm-we're saying the same thing. I didn't know you noticed. Actually, I have a surprise for you tomorrow morning."

Riley's face lit up. "A surprise for me? What is it?"

Ron chuckled. "If I told you, it won't be a surprise anymore." He glanced at the bar. "I need a drink. What's your poison of choice?"

"Poison. Something *really* strong. I want to get trashed."

When a woman says something like that to a man, his reptile brain is overstimulated. Ron's cock twitched. He really was changing. The old Ron would have been concerned for her. Right now, all he saw was the opportunity.

"Any ideas?" asked Riley.

"I'm getting rum and Coke for myself. Rum and orange juice okay for you? More rum than orange?"

"Perfect."

"I'll be right back. Don't vanish on me."

Riley smiled and batted her eyelids. "I won't."

At the bar, Ron went to the opposite end, away from Wyatt and Claudia. The bar was busier now, and he joined a line of people waiting for their turn. More people had shown up as the night progressed.

When it got to his turn, to avoid rejoining the line soon, Ron asked the bartender to put three drinks each in a large enough glass. She looked at him, then shrugged. He left her a ten dollar tip and walked back with two glasses, one orange, the other dark brown.

"Big, this looks good," said Riley. She raised her full glass, and soon it was half empty. Riley licked her lips, blinked, and cleared her throat. "Wow, strong shit."

"Umm…I better warn you, there are three drinks in there," said Ron. "You might want to sip it slowly. There was a line, and I know we'll be needing more soon."

Riley belched loudly, then giggled. "That's fine. It hit the spot. I'll sip moving forward."

"Have you been looking at the pictures I've been sending? Any favorites?"

Riley slapped her forehead. "Sorry I forgot. I'll take a look." Then she leaned forward. "Do you know I've been modeling since I was eight years old?"

"No, that young?"

"Yes. My mom signed me up for a tryout, and they selected me. Since then, it was one photoshoot after another. Not all made money, but they were all demanding. Sometimes I was pulled out of school for weeks. My childhood was spent in one studio or the other."

Ron took a long drink from his glass. He wasn't sure he wanted to hear Riley's story, but the alcohol had loosened something in her. In the background, *Stronger* by Kelly Clarkson started to play.

"I love that song! Come on, let's dance." Riley grabbed Ron's hand.

Ron didn't want to dance, but it looked like the song had a special meaning for her from what she'd said so far. He got to his feet, and they ran to the dance floor.

They danced to that one, the next song that came up, and the next one. They only went back to their seat when the DJ played *Jingle Bells*.

"Darn, our table has been taken," said Riley as they walked back.

Ron looked to make sure his coat was still draped over the chair. The couple occupying their seats got up as they approached. The man said he'd seen them when they left to dance. They could have their table back.

"Thanks," said Ron with a nod. He looked at the bar; the line was gone. Their drinks were still there on the table, but anything could have happened to them. "I'm thirsty, you want another drink?"

Claudia fanned herself with her hand. "Yes, please. And in a big glass." Riley's eyes glowed. She looked happy, the earlier sadness gone.

At the bar, there was no sign of Wyatt or Claudia. Ron looked around and spotted them on the dance floor, and they were dirty dancing. He smiled, ordered their drinks, and went back to Riley. She, too, was watching the dance floor. This time she didn't look sad.

Ron handed Riley her drink.

"Thank you." Riley smiled at him and took a sip. "Do you think they're in love?"

She couldn't be talking about Wyatt and Claudia. "Who?"

"Look at the couples dancing. Which ones do you think are in love?"

Ron laughed nervously. "I'm no love expert." He didn't know where this was going, but he knew someone not on the dance floor was in love or at least liked someone on the dance floor. To avoid answering any more questions, he raised his glass and started to drink.

Riley drained hers. "Drink up and let's go dance some more."

Ron gulped down his drink. The alcohol started to take hold. He and Riley danced to popular dance music, slow jams, and Christmas songs too. He didn't even know when Claudia and Wyatt left, but it was getting close to midnight, and both he and Riley were slurring their words.

"We'd better leave now that we can still walk," said Riley.

"I agree, but I have to get my coat." Ron got his coat. "I'll walk you to your room, okay?" They walked hand in hand out of the lounge and into the hallway.

"Wow, that's loud silence out here," said Riley. "And it's kind of cold."

Ron took off his coat and placed it over her shoulders. Riley looked up at him, smiled, and put her head on his shoulder. Slowly, they headed down the hall toward her room and arrived at her door.

Riley looked up and stared at him, and slowly their lips came closer and closer.

Ron's pulse raced. He'd been trying to get close to Riley, and suddenly there she was, within his grasp. Their lips touched, and soon they were kissing hard.

Riley moaned like a puppy as they kissed, pushing her tongue into his. Her body pressed flush against him.

Ron drew back and looked at Riley. Her hard nipples looked like spikes in her dress, trying to poke through. He cupped her ass and squeezed. And their lips found each other again.

This time, Riley broke free. Chest heaving, eyes glazed, she fished inside her purse, produced her room key, and handed it to Ron.

Ron knew he was in a situation where his values could be compromised or her values could be trashed. He would blame it on the alcohol. He unlocked the door and let them in.

40

THEY ATTACKED EACH OTHER WITH RAW ANIMAL INSTINCT. Ron was not thinking. All he wanted to do was embed his cock inside her where it belonged. They stumbled toward the bed, and Ron kicked off his shoes and began unbuttoning his shirt, his lips glued to hers.

Riley pulled back and raised both hands. "Take it off."

Ron obliged. He lowered himself to his haunches, grabbed the hem of her dress at the ankle, and brushed his face against her leg, sniffing like a hound as he came up, then his breath caught. He smelled perfume mixed with pure female musk, and he felt his cock grow harder.

"Jesus!" Riley had no underwear on. He continued lifting her dress up, rubbing his nose against the tuft of landing airstrip between her legs and inhaling deeply.

Riley's body reminded him of Tyra Banks on the cover of Sports Illustrated sans bikini top and bottom. Tits, slim waist, and a curvy ass. In addition to no panties, Riley wasn't wearing a bra. No wonder her nipples looked like arrowheads poking at her gown from the inside.

Once Ron stood erect, her hands were on his belt, fumbling as if she was still learning how to unbuckle a guy's belt. Ron removed her hand and undid it himself before tossing his pants aside.

Riley dropped to her knees and grabbed his cock. Shaky laughter bubbled out of her. "Oh my God. It's *huge*." She held it awkwardly, barely able to wrap her hand around its girth. "I feel it getting bigger in my hand." She looked at him with dewy eyes, as if waiting for instructions on what to do next. She stuck out her tongue and gave his knob a lick as if it were a lollipop.

Ron was amused. It seemed like Riley wasn't experienced at giving blow jobs. But a feminine touch was a feminine touch. His dick was steel.

Riley backed away to the bed, lay on her back, and spread her legs wide. She issued her first command. "Eat it."

Ron didn't need to be told twice. He brushed her thigh with the back of his fingers and was rewarded with a shaking of her legs. He went straight for gold and landed on her mound, brushing his thumb over her clit.

Riley's body shivered, and a deep moan escaped her throat. "Yes." Her thighs quivered, and she dug her fingers into his hair.

Ron wanted a taste of that pussy. He came closer and noticed writing above the landing strip tuft of pubic hair. Written in black cursive tattoo was *Mary's*. *Mary owns this pussy?* Well, not tonight. Tonight, it was Ron's pussy. He raided her vagina like a hoard of marauding Vikings - licking, poking, nibbling, and stroking. She tasted sweet.

Riley thrashed around like she was on fire, trying to roll over and snuff out the flames, moaning with each movement.

She grabbed his head and literally tried to shove his face into her.

Ron figured out she wanted up and down strokes, and he was duty-bound to serve. He stuck his tongue out and brushed up and down her core, and soon Riley was grunting and groaning, warning him of her impending orgasm. Then suddenly, her body went rigid. "I…I came," she said breathlessly, her chest rising and falling with each breath. "I came."

Ron came up for air, her sweetness fresh on his tongue. His nose, mouth, and face were sleek and sticky with her juices. He stroked his cock, excited by her response and ready to fill her up. He positioned himself between her legs, rubbed her core with the knob of his cock, then dipped it in. It came out slick and shiny.

"Please, Ron, fuck me."

Ron nearly came. *God.* He pushed his cock in slowly, savoring every moment. He lowered his lips and kissed her. Her hands were on his back, digging in. He felt her body go tense as he pushed in. Ron stopped, drew back, and embedded his cock deep to the base with one quick thrust.

Riley gasped. Her fingers dug into his back, ripping his skin.

Ron pushed in and out. The pain on his back and pleasure from his cock blended into one. "You're so tight," he managed, his voice wound like a coiled spring. He drove into her faster and harder. Her pussy gripped him like a vise, just allowing the slightest of movement. The sensation was too much. Ron came, grunting and shaking like a hand holding a selfie stick for five minutes.

Eyes shut tight, mouth open, feet flapping on the bed, he lay on her panting, both of them breathing hard. Ron had never come that hard before. He raised himself to his elbows as his breathing came under control. That was when he noticed the tears streaming down Riley's cheeks.

"Riley, you're crying. What is it? Are you hurt?" *It was consensual, right?* He wasn't sure. No papers were signed.

"Do you love me?"

"What?" Ron didn't know what to say. He used to worship her, but now he wasn't so sure. There was Claudia… He was in a position that demanded he yelled out *yes*, but he didn't want to deceive her. His dick shrank and popped out of her.

Riley wiped her eyes and smiled. "Let me make it easier for you. I don't love you." She stretched out her hand to the bedside table and grabbed the box of tissue there. "There will be blood." She handed it to Ron. "I'm so sore."

Ron took the tissue box and pulled out a few. He wiped himself, and it came out red. His head jerked up. It all made sense to him now. "You're a virgin? My God, you used me."

"I'm very sorry, let me explain."

41

WYATT

WYATT HAD GONE BEYOND HIS CAPACITY FOR MANHATTANS. He was past buzzed and headed toward tipsy. Horny as hell, he was confident he could bend Claudia over on the bar and take her right there.

Just then, Claudia wrapped her lips around his ear lobe and whispered, "Let's take it to my room."

The effect on him was like someone had tied a string around his cock and yanked. He hustled her off the dance floor, out of the lounge and down the hall. Now they were in her room, and his cock was engorged, threatening to blow a fuse.

Claudia led him toward the couch in her room.

They should be heading to the bed, thought Wyatt, but his dick was all positive thoughts. As long as whatever she had planned would end in him getting some attention, he didn't mind.

"Take your shirt off," said Claudia.

Wyatt's fingers rushed to his shirt. He unbuttoned the first two buttons while the third gave him a hard time. He pulled it over his head as he would a T-shirt. When he looked at Claudia, all he noticed were boobs. She'd slipped her dress off at the shoulders, and it was bunched up around her waist.

"Claudia."

She raised her eyebrows in a *What is it? Don't you see I'm busy l*ook? Claudia pulled at each of his nipples until they were rock hard.

Each time his nipple was stroked, it felt like a jolt of lightning wrapped in pleasure traveling all the way to his balls.

Claudia's eyes were fixed on his as she started to undo his pants.

His heart pounded in anticipation. He was literally standing on his tiptoes, waiting for what she would do to him. His pants came down. The coolness he felt confirmed that he wasn't dreaming. His needs would be attended to soon. She pushed her fingers into his boxers, and soon those were wrapped around his ankles.

Shoot me now! Wyatt's cock hung in the air like an angler's rod with a big fish, putting a lot of pressure on it.

Claudia licked her lips and murmured to herself, "Okay, where do we start?" She leaned forward and, without touching Wyatt, took his whole knob in her mouth. She pulled it out with a pop and smacked her lips. "A little salty."

Wyatt threw his head back. "My God." The visual was just insane. But she wasn't done. She opened her mouth wide, leaned forward, and his pride and joy vanished down her throat. Her nose was buried in his pubic hair, and his sac looked like a bag of nuts under her chin. She reached for them, hefted them in her palms, and rolled them about as if they were stress balls.

Right away his sac tightened, even though her finger was delicate, just applying the right amount of pressure.

Claudia pulled her head back, and Wyatt's cock reappeared slick with saliva. She gasped for air, then repeated the performance. When she pulled back a second time after catching her breath, she started to bob her head over his knob, making sucking sounds.

"Oh shit. Oh fuck." Wyatt felt the lips of pleasure grip him. There was a difference in sensation between a mouth and pussy. Right now, Wyatt couldn't string together the right combination of words to describe it. But he knew Claudia's mouth was the bomb.

Claudia did not relent. She worked his cock in and out of her mouth. Using her lips, tongue, and suction power to create a sensation the vagina would call *showing off*.

Right now, Wyatt was laying up for a slam dunk. "Fuck shit, I'm going to explode."

Suddenly in the middle of all that craziness, he saw the door open, and a figure stepped in. Wyatt didn't know whether it was the Manhattans working overtime or if it was an apparition.

Still, he remained on that trajectory to orgasm when he recognized Ron, his former roommate. *What the...?* Ron started to approach, and Wyatt was thrown off course.

42

CAMERON

RON CAME BACK FROM THE BATHROOM WHERE HE'D WET A towel and cleaned himself up. He was now wearing his boxers, pants, and shoes, walking around, looking for where he'd tossed his shirt.

"You're a handsome guy, you know that, right?" said Riley. She wore a bathrobe and had complained a few times that her vagina was sore.

Ron shook his head and laughed. "I still can't believe you used me."

"That's why nothing ever happened. I knew you were a nice guy, but I love Mary. I won't be able to love you back. It was all that rum that made me actually do it."

"It was good. I didn't know you were a virgin. It would have affected my performance. But you were so tight. I don't mind a no strings attached fuck now and then."

Red blotches appeared on Riley's cheeks. "That's what

you say now, but it's human nature to always want more. I don't have any more love to give. Mary has it all."

"I would never have guessed you and Mary were a couple."

"Because she's my agent?"

"Well, yeah. Mary has a legitimate reason to be around you and fuss over you. Being twenty years older than you, it looked normal. I mean, as long as you are working, she gets a cut. So people think her show of affection is her protecting her interest."

Riley sat on the bed, her coat open, and showed the bulge of her panties she'd stuffed with sanitary pads. "Remember, I told you my mother got me started in modeling."

Ron nodded. "Yeah."

"My mother would drop me off at the studio and leave. Soon others noticed I didn't have adult supervision around me apart from the photographers who, when they're not working with you, are working with someone else."

Ron picked up his shirt from the garbage. "They can't really watch you." *How did it get there?* He shook it off and put it on.

"It didn't take long before the abuse started." She patted her underwear and fixed her bathrobe to stop flashing.

"Oh my God. Did you tell your parents?"

Riley laughed. "My father used my mom as a punching bag. One time she called the cops on him but refused to press charges. The next day, he packed a suitcase and left."

"You must have told your mom. What did she say?"

"She said I was now our meal ticket. I should suck it up or the photographers would stop using me for shoots."

Anger boiled inside Ron. He knew there were predators out there, but preying on a child… "Do you have names? You can still go after them."

"Well, Mary was a model too, and always stood up to people trying to take advantage of me. She would ask me why my parents weren't there with me, and I told her my dad left, and Mom only cared about the money. She could relate. Had a similar experience as me. She soon showed up at the same shoots as me, even when she didn't have any work with them, just to protect me. At sixteen, I petitioned the court. I made a lot of money, but my mother spent it on her drug habit. Once I got emancipated, I lived on my own, managing my finances."

"Aha," said Ron with a smile. "She's a predator."

"No, we hung out together, and on my twenty-first birthday, she treated me to a European vacation, and that's when we started dating."

Ron sighed and sat on the bed beside her. "You should have told me all this. I wouldn't have had my hopes up."

"No, Ron. Like I said, I like you a lot. In fact, Mary and I are thinking of having a baby." Riley shrugged. "You know, she's almost fifty, so we decided I would be the biological mother to minimize risks."

Ron nodded.

Riley continued. "Mary used to be heterosexual, so we agreed it would be a good idea for me to experience a man too before we started a family. I picked you after we started working together. Then I figured you liked me. Maybe more than that, which would make it hard to get rid of you. I was going to seduce you here in Mountain Peak anyway."

There was silence. "So what made you change your mind?"

"I saw Wyatt. I remembered him as the conceited skiing champion from college. We would have sex and go our separate ways. But he seemed to have changed too. In his college days, he banged anything that moved."

Ron nodded. "Yep, he was my roommate."

"Now he wouldn't come close to me in that sense. I tried to get him away from Claudia, but she seemed to have stolen his mind."

Ron's mind drifted to Claudia. *Where was she?*

"Even you too."

Ron looked Riley. "Me?"

"I think you've fallen for her too."

"Claudia?" said Ron.

"Yes. I see it in your eyes. And she likes you too. She'll have to choose between you and Wyatt." Riley inhaled and exhaled. "There's something about Claudia. What about her fascinates you?"

Ron exhaled. "I don't know, but I can relate to her story."

"Which is?"

"Since she was eight, she'd been blaming herself for her mother's death."

Riley's hands flew to her lips. "Oh no. What happened?"

"She threw a tantrum on her birthday. She wanted unicorn candles for her cake and sent her mother to get them. She got in an accident with a semi. Her mother died on her birthday because she threw a tantrum." Ron had a painful lump in his throat. "That got me."

"Poor girl, that's terrible."

Right then, Ron knew he had to go find her. He was also concerned. He wanted to bring kids into this world under his own terms. "Umm...Riley, you...you're not by any chance ovulating?"

She threw her head back and laughed. "I've always heard that men's dicks have a mind of their own. Why don't you come back when I'm less sore? I like the way you feel me up."

The back of Ron's neck felt incredibly hot. "We'll see about that. I have to go."

Ron stepped out of Riley's room and walked down the corridor briskly towards Claudia's room. The time on his phone said almost 2:00 am. It was late, and she was probably sleeping.

He stopped at her door, raised his hand to knock, then saw the key in the keyhole. He knew that key from last night. One thing flashed through his mind. *Is she safe?* Ron's heart started to pound in his chest. He took a deep breath and opened the door slowly.

Claudia was on her knees, her face hanging over Wyatt's crotch. She must have heard him because she turned around, and Wyatt's cock popped out of her mouth. Their eyes connected.

43

Claudia

CLAUDIA COULDN'T BELIEVE SHE WAS ON HER KNEES WITH Wyatt's cock in her mouth. The night had turned out as she'd expected, perhaps better. All that hard work finally paid off. The body-hugging black dress, Ron's gift to her, was a killer. Wyatt was literally drooling when he saw her in it. And that cock stealing bitch, Riley, was put in her place.

The smell of his sweaty balls was like walking into the locker room of a hockey team after a game. It got her girly parts giving up their juices over her thong and seeping through to the black dress.

Claudia couldn't believe she'd succeeded in fucking all three boys, her boys within the same thirty-six hours. That was like one guy a day! She would ride Wyatt instead of blowing him so there wouldn't be any doubt. She didn't know how liking three men at the same time would work out, but she'd better make it a trifecta while she was still ahead. Claudia pulled his cock out of her mouth.

"Please don't stop," said Wyatt, breathless.

"To the bed," said Claudia.

Wyatt turned and scrambled up the bed faster than a monkey pursued by baboons. He propped up some pillows and threw himself on them, his cock at full mast.

A thought came to Claudia. She turned around and hitched up her dress over her waist and imagined what her butt cheeks would look like just separated by a thong.

Wyatt groaned, grabbed her hips, and pulled her toward him.

Claudia giggled, vindicated by his response. She gasped as his cock filled her up from the back. She wasn't used to taking him in from that angle, and she rode him cowgirl style. Claudia moaned as bolts of pleasure cascaded all over her body. She was about to get undone, but not yet. She fought it, staved it off, and managed to climb off him, all shaky. Soon her lips were on his cock, licking herself off him.

"Oh, Claudia," said Wyatt and growled like an animal.

As Claudia basked in Wyatt's now verbal approval was added to the mix, she thought she heard the door open behind her. Of course, she'd left the key in the lock. But to her surprise, she didn't pull away or try to hide. After all, this was her room. Perhaps the daiquiris had helped chip away at her inhibitions. Whoever it was would have one hell of a view with her thong-clad butt up in the air, her sex open, dripping and inviting.

She didn't let up on Wyatt's cock. His abs had gone tense, his thigh muscles rigid, and his breathing was coming in gasps. She knew that sign and would be rewarded soon. But curiosity got the better of her. She turned behind to look and couldn't believe her eyes. It was Ron, her Ron.

Her mind went straight to the gutter. The thought of

having both of her boys fill her up materialized from nowhere.

She sensed a change in Wyatt. His cock seemed to partially deflate in her hands. She knew the story - Wyatt had slept with Ron's girlfriend in college.

Wyatt sat up. "What the…?"

Claudia raised herself to her knees. She placed her palm on Wyatt's chest and gently pushed him back. His heartbeat felt like a bird caught in a hunter's net, trying to escape.

The tension-filled moment excited Claudia. She squeezed Wyatt's cock with her right hand and caressed his nipple with her hand on his chest. "It's okay," she cooed. "It's okay." She sucked his knob with a loud, sucking sound. "You have me already."

Wyatt let out a deep breath.

Claudia felt the tension leave his body.

Wyatt fell back on the pillow and covered his eyes with his elbow and whispered, "Please, don't stop."

Claudia's heart pounded in her chest like galloping horses. Her whole body hummed with excitement. She waved Ron forward. Her dress had covered her butt when she raised herself, so she hitched it up, exposing her ass.

Claudia went back to sucking Wyatt, and soon she heard buckle and zipper being opened, and the rustle of fabric. Moments later, cold clammy hands landed on her bare ass cheeks. Fingers pried at her thong and shifted it to one side.

Claudia felt Ron's cock poke around her core. She knew her pussy was flooded, ready to receive. Once he found-

"Huh," gasped Claudia, almost gagging on Wyatt's dick as Ron's cock slid into her. By the second thrust of Ron's cock, she was undone, and a mind-blowing orgasm ripped through her body.

She didn't have time to recover. Ron pounded away

behind her, pushing her forward each time he drove into her, driving Wyatt's cock deeper down her throat.

Quickly, Claudia found a rhythm, taking Wyatt in deep with every thrust from Ron. They formed a well-oiled fucking machine.

Wyatt was now gasping for air, thrusting and moving his hips. His palms were now face down on the sheet, his fingers poking into them.

Claudia stole a look at Wyatt; his eyes were shut tight. A sound like a truck going uphill at a high gear spewed from his throat. Behind her, the *slap slap slap* sound of flesh smacking flesh filled the room.

"I'm coming," announced Wyatt. He tried to pull his cock out of Claudia's mouth, but she knocked his hand away. Claudia grabbed his butt and pulled him closer. With a loud grunt, Wyatt shuddered, and his hot cum hit the back of her throat. She didn't let him out until she'd sucked him dry.

"Jesus…Jesus," whispered Wyatt as if he'd found religion.

Claudia found herself climbing up the hill again, heading toward the edge with Ron thrusting away behind her.

Her whole body tingled. She felt lightheaded, her vision dipping at the sides before becoming blurry. An amazing sensation that left her tongue-tied sprang from her clit and spread all over her body. She was at the hilltop, on edge. Her body spun, and she seemed to dip in and out of blackness.

Ron's fingers dug into her ass; she was sure he was going to leave bruises. He plunged in one more time, leaned forward, and whispered in Claudia's ear, "I'm about to explode." His whole body started to shake.

Claudia felt him get bigger inside her. An explosion seemed to take place inside the confines of her core. She came undone, and a loud scream escaped her lips as Ron came inside her. She collapsed on top of Wyatt, panting.

As the fog and cobweb of her climax cleared, reality kicked in. Claudia asked herself, *What have I done?*

She was sandwiched between two men who hated each other's guts. Was it a good thing she had united them? Had she brought them together? Her body was still wracked by tremors, but she felt Ron get off her, heard his zipper go up, and then the sound of his belt buckle. Moments later, she heard the door shut. It probably was the best thing.

Wyatt had covered his eyes again with his elbow. *Shame?* Claudia couldn't answer that. She knew neither Wyatt and Ron were gay, but she would never know how they felt about coming seconds apart while connected to the same woman. For her, it was exhilarating.

She flopped on her back beside Wyatt and pulled her dress down. Claudia felt satisfied, having given as much as she'd gotten. She pulled the covers over herself and soon drifted off to sleep with a smile on her lips.

44

Claudia

A COLD WIND WHISTLED PAST CLAUDIA'S EARS AS SHE STOOD
with Wyatt and Riley at the bottom of Deer Edge Slope. The
sun was up, causing everything in its path to dazzle, including
the cordoned-off Devils Edge, extending further down
beyond Deer Edge Slope.

It was early in the morning, and people were just heading
out to their events for the day. In the distance, the lift became
operational, and folks were lining up for the next car up the
hill.

Only Claudia *really* knew why they were there. The
instructors, she and Wyatt, were supposed to meet up with
Max, but Riley had come along because of Wyatt.

"I wonder what news Max will bring this time?" said
Wyatt.

Riley chuckled. "Don't worry, you'll find out soon."

Claudia unclipped herself from her skis and looked
around. A small group of vacationers walked past them. One

of them had a sweater that actually said *Ugliest Christmas Sweater*. It was indeed ugly. Claudia smiled, recalling that her sister Holly had introduced an ugly Christmas sweater line where she worked. Well, she owned part of the company now.

Another one of them had a sandwich and a Thermos that obviously contained coffee because they were overwhelmed by its smell. Claudia guessed his sandwich had bacon in it. She could do with coffee, but no food. Wyatt had filled her up last night. It still seemed like a dream to Claudia. She'd had Wyatt and Ron at the same time

It suddenly felt hot inside her ski gear. Claudia still marveled at how she was able to pull last night off. She hadn't planned it. The only thing contrived was getting Wyatt to abandon Riley, which Wyatt did with Ron's help. But now, she had fallen for Ron too.

Claudia glanced at Riley; she didn't seem rattled at all. Carefree, no worries. She would peek at Wyatt, then look away. And occasionally, she would look around. *Looking for Ron?*

Claudia had caught Wyatt looking at her with a longing in his eyes. Has he *really* fallen for her too? Oh goodness, things were getting complicated. And there was Max also. "Shit," said Claudia under her breath. She was literally at the center of this debacle.

Just then, she looked up the slope and saw Ron's blue coat racing down the hill. Claudia giggled, clapped her hands together, and jumped up and down.

"Is that Ron?" asked Riley, taking a step closer. "Oh my God, it is Ron!"

Claudia smiled. Ron came down fast with perfect form and excellent coordination.

Wyatt had the beginning of a smile on his lips. "He must

have been practicing." He gave Claudia a quick look and then returned his gaze to Ron. Wyatt dug his poles into the snow, folded his arms, and continued to watch.

It's incredible how fast people travel on skis. Moments later, he headed toward the group and sprayed them with snow.

Claudia smiled. She knew that Ron would walk into her arms once he got off his skis.

"Ron! Ron!" screamed Riley. "You did it!"

Ron pushed off toward her, and Riley ran into his arms. They hugged like lost long friends.

Disappointment washed over Claudia. Well, at least she'd lived up to her own part of the deal. He had impressed Riley, and as things seemed, won her over. She let out a shaky breath. *Jesus, Claudia, you want to have all the men to yourself?* Ron was too good for her. But if that's what he wanted, then that's what he wanted. She turned away, suddenly beset by a feeling that she was going to be sick. Her stomach clenched, and she felt like she was shrinking.

"Claudia!"

Startled, Claudia whirled around and looked into Ron's smiling face.

"This is for you!" shouted Ron and kicked off on his skis.

Claudia smiled. She got him. Then her smile faded as she realized what he was doing. He was headed for Devils Edge. An avalanche had turned that slope into a table. You didn't see it until you were airborne. "Oh God. He's going to kill himself."

"What's he doing?" blurted Wyatt.

"Wyatt, please, please stop him," pleaded Claudia. "You're the only one quick enough to stop him."

Wyatt looked at Ron as he gathered speed. Then beyond at the expanse of snow where he might meet his end.

"Please, Wyatt," she whispered. "For me."

45

W YATT

"JESUS CHRIST!" BARKED WYATT. "THERE'S NO NEED TO kill myself as well, Claudia. I might as well just hold hands with him and go over the edge, for Christ's sake."

Claudia's eyes brimming with tears.

A quick calculation went through Wyatt's mind. Ron going over the edge would eliminate any opposition. Claudia would be all his. But those eyes would never look at him the same. He was in love with her, and anything, like her mother's death, that would put sorrow in her heart would destroy him too. Letting Ron off himself would put her in such a state. Then it would be too late. He wouldn't be able to help. The only help he could provide was now.

Claudia whimpered. "Please."

And she was right too. Only he had the speed to cut Ron off. That is, if he moved right now. "Fuck! Fuck!" Wyatt snapped his goggles in place and pushed off after Ron.

Wyatt was thankful for the back and core exercises he'd

maintained over the years. Ron had almost half a minute head start, but skill mattered, and Wyatt was sure he could catch up. Once he gathered speed, he dropped into a tuck, pointed his skis straight downhill, and took off like a bullet.

Within seconds he ate up the distance between him and Ron. He looked ahead and saw the drop and felt his balls contract. How was he going to stop Ron? He could overtake him, but that didn't mean Ron would stop. He might think it was a race and try to save face by moving faster. Or ram Wyatt, and they both would roll over the cliff.

The other alternative would be to get Ron's attention and point him away from danger. The latter sounded like the best move, and he hoped Ron would understand and not act contrary to the plan.

Wyatt was now abreast of Ron, and they were close to the edge. Air rushed past his ears like a dragon spitting cold fire.

"Ron! Ron!"

At the speed they were going, the wind snatched the words out of Wyatt's mouth. Wyatt's only hope was that Ron would see him in his periphery. He watched Ron.

The way Ron skied, he could have been on a simulator in his living room, practicing skiing 101. Then, Wyatt's wish was granted.

Ron turned to his right, saw Wyatt, and immediately lost control. He wobbled and headed toward Wyatt.

Wyatt had expected that and moved away. It was like dodging a car that has strayed into your lane on the highway. He watched as Ron fought, regained control and did the opposite of what Wyatt hoped he would do. He moved away from Wyatt, digging his poles into the snow, propelling himself toward the edge.

"Fuck!" *Think think*, Wyatt demanded of himself. His eyes were on Ron, and he could imagine what was going through his head. At a comfortable speed, Ron would look around to see if he'd lost Wyatt. And when he saw Wyatt or perhaps the edge, whichever came first, he would lose control.

They were close to the edge, and Wyatt knew sometimes there was no ground under such edges. It could only be held up by ice and luck. His heart was in his throat. He expected the bottom to fall out from underneath them at any moment. He could ski away and save himself.

Ron must have noticed the drop because Wyatt sensed when Ron lost control, and everything he'd learned seemed to desert him.

Ron was on a sure path over the edge, like a heat-seeking missile locked on a target. Ron's target was the cliff edge.

Wyatt's only option was a snatch and run.

"Go limp, Ron! Go limp!" Wyatt dropped his left pole and moved closer to Ron. He extended his hand like he was about to hug him, then encircled Ron's torso from behind him and pulled Ron toward his body in one swift swoop. The execution was perfect.

Ron was no featherweight and fell into Wyatt, knocking him off his skis. Together they hit the snow hard, tumbling and rolling away from the edge.

There was a loud crack, followed by a tremendous roar, and the ground rumbled. Tons of snow started to move.

Wyatt gulped in air, hoping he would have enough to survive when tons of snow descended on them. His heartbeat thundered in his chest like a gorilla rattling its cage. He waited for the inevitable. For snow to heap all over them. Instead, all he heard was silence.

Moments later, the unmistakable sound of a snowmobile reached his ears. Then voices.

"I can see them!" said a male voice.

Wyatt felt movement beside him. "Ron…are you okay?"

Ron coughed. "I think so."

Wyatt raised his head, then lifted himself up. The wind whirled snow around him like white dust, and he saw that the distance from the edge was now closer. He looked up and saw Max Steel get off a snowmobile and run toward them.

"Wyatt! Ron! Are you guys all right?"

Wyatt smiled.

They'd made it.

It was a miracle they'd survived. Behind Max was Claudia. Sweet Claudia coming to their aid, her face as white as the ground underneath them.

"Yes," said Ron with a groan.

Wyatt got up and brushed snow away from his clothing. "I think so."

"Come on, guys," said Max, helping Ron up. "Let's move farther away from the edge. We don't know how stable this platform is."

Claudia ran up to Max and Wyatt. "Thank goodness you're okay."

"Take him to the snowmobile," said Max. "I'll give Ron a hand."

Wyatt locked eyes with Claudia.

She mouthed *thank you* and gave him a hug, holding him tight.

Wyatt buried his face in her hair and inhaled. Her smell reminded him of last night. Heat spread all over his body. "I'm fine. Go see if Ron needs help." Wyatt walked over to the snow vehicles as more people arrived. He heard Claudia speak to Ron.

"Ron…are you all right?" asked Claudia.

Ron moved his wrist. "I think so - all thanks to Wyatt."

Claudia touched his shoulder. "I was so worried. What… what made you do such a reckless thing?"

Ron looked around. His eyes drifted from Max to Ron, then back to Claudia. He exhaled. "You…I wanted to impress you. I needed you to choose me. I wanted to do something desperate before." He looked at Wyatt. "Before it was too late, and I lost you."

"Oh Ron. I…" Claudia's voice trailed off.

The wind howled around them, the silence punctuated by the sound of other rescuers getting closer and closer. Max broke it.

"Choose you for what?" asked Max, furrowing his forehead.

Wyatt glanced at Max, and almost immediately, it seemed like an understanding came to him. Blood drained from his face, and he did a full circle as he looked from Wyatt to Ron, and then to Claudia.

"You have to choose, Claudia," said Wyatt, pulling his eyes away from Max. He lowered his voice as he added, "Before somebody gets killed."

"What the fuck are you guys still doing here?" It was one of the older admin guys. "Having a party? Get moving! This platform might still be unstable. And there's a blizzard coming this way too. It's definitely going to be a white Christmas for everybody. Move it! Move it!" He leaned closer to Max. "Come on, Steel, you should know better."

46

Claudia

THE DAY'S ACTIVITIES CONTINUED, BUT BECAUSE IT WAS Christmas Eve, all coaching ended by noon at the resort. From then on, it would be one party after the other at the lounge until New Year's countdown in a few days.

The day had ended abruptly for Claudia and the guys, with what was called a minor avalanche by the local news crew. They had no idea what they were saying. Claudia had created a major disturbance in the lives of these three men, whose only crime was opening their hearts to her.

Claudia lay on her bed in her room at the resort, deep in thought. Her bed reeked of sex, and thinking about how it got that way wasn't helping her predicament.

She'd managed to get Max, Ron, and Wyatt involved with her. Ron nearly killed himself and Wyatt by trying to prove himself. It wasn't fair to any of them. She must choose.

Claudia understood how they felt. Like when she lost her mother. She longed for something she couldn't have. The yearning had gone on since then. She had to do something fast. She didn't think she could survive the guilt of being responsible for another person's death. This morning it could have been two. She had to choose before there was another repeat of this morning. It was a tough decision. She loved all three of them.

Claudia needed someone to talk to. Someone to help her decide. She wished Jane were still here, but she'd gone home for Christmas. She and her boyfriend were spending time with her family.

The other people she could talk to were her sisters or Aunt Sam. Claudia's face, neck, and ears burned with heat. How do you tell your family you slept with three men in thirty-six hours?

She could see Nicole's mortified face. "You should have come to me if you needed money. You don't have to sell your body."

Laughter bubbled in Claudia's stomach and burst out of her lips before she could stop it. Her decision would have been simple if she'd slept with them just for money. The relief she got from the laugher faded, and she was back to the problems she faced.

Claudia's phone buzzed. It was an incoming message from Max, and he wanted to see her. Earlier, she'd also gotten texts from Ron and Wyatt. They all wanted to meet. The constant communication with them wasn't helping her reach a decision.

Claudia sent them a text to meet her in her room at 1:00 pm. The time on her phone was just shy of 12:30. She put her phone in the drawer beside the bed. Out of sight, out of mind.

Each of her boys had a different aspect of them that she admired. Ron, a successful photographer, was like the boy next door. The high school sweetheart she never had. Wyatt was the closest thing to a handsome celebrity you wouldn't mind getting your hands on. Maybe he was an asshole, but the Wyatt she'd met was different. He hadn't lied to her about Riley—they were not a thing—and she too had left. And Wyatt had saved Ron because she'd asked him to. A lump formed in her throat as she remembered the look he'd given her before he went after Ron.

Then there was Max, a soldier of fortune by circumstance. How many women out there have had a crush on an older guy when they were younger, and later had the chance to be with their crush, now older and even better, and they rejected it? Nobody.

Max had shown her a different side of Mountain Peak, like the night sky and Fox Run Ridge. Introducing her to Bradford, the wonderful old man. She wondered how his trip to see his sister was going.

Claudia sat up straight. Bradford said she could come and visit anytime, whether he was there or not. She swung off the bed and started to dress up as warm as she could. She would visit the cottage. The serenity alone would give her the peace of mind to think.

"Where is it?" said Claudia out loud. She'd had her phone in her hand seconds ago. Claudia needed to get out of the room before the guys arrived and met her. She had no answer for them yet.

Claudia remembered she would need snowshoes. She went to the cabin where the snowmobiles were stored and got herself snowshoes and a compass.

Then she rushed off to her car. A few flurries floated in the air as she gunned her car, heading for Fox Run Ridge.

Out of habit, she reached for her phone on the passenger seat. "Shit." She turned on the radio and listened to Christmas carols. Then the news came. The local report was urging people to finish their shopping as early as possible and stay indoors.

NEWSCASTER

"About 5-10" of snow will be dumped on the vicinity overnight, in addition to the 4" already on the ground." The newscaster chuckled. "Whoever is praying for a white Christmas should stop now. We have more than enough! The information-"

CLAUDIA CHANGED THE CHANNEL AS SHE DROVE PAST MAIN Street, which was full of Christmas shoppers and vacationers. It amazed her how all these people vanished after the New Year and the town was reduced to its normal inhabitants. The cycle would start all over again.

Once past Main Street, she gunned the Accord uphill, hoping she wouldn't, by some strange twist of fate, run into Max. She needed a clear head to think about this. Thinking about her situation, she was leaning toward Ron. Was it because he was the last of the guys to fall for her?

Then Wyatt. It was pure love for her that made him go after Ron. She could have lost both. Claudia exhaled as she turned into the Fox Run parking.

One minute there are flurries, the next they'd stopped falling. Maybe the weatherman had gotten it wrong. Claudia parked the car, put on her snowshoes, and exited the vehicle. She started to retrace the path she and Max had taken that day.

The landmarks she recalled from memory, and it was easy to follow. Claudia felt it was a bit faster too. This time, there was no sightseeing or someone to talk to. It was straight trudging through the snow.

The flurries, now turned into snow, came down like an all-white confetti explosion. Visibility was still adequate, but Claudia began to worry that the snow would get heavier before she got to the cottage.

She sniffed the air, hoping to catch a whiff of smoke coming from the old man's chimney, but there was nothing. She should be happy. At least it confirmed that nobody was there.

Behind her, the falling snow covered the patterns made by her snowshoes. That could be a problem going back. Claudia chuckled. If she had crumbs, she would have dropped them like Hansel and Gretel.

Claudia continued, and when she passed a ridge, she saw the cottage. A slow smile stretched her lips. There were no prints on the snow, no sign of life. She walked over to the birdfeeder, pulled out the drawer, and saw that the key was there as if she'd put it there herself.

Claudia unlocked the door and stepped in. It was cold. A far cry from the day she'd come with Max. Somehow in her mind, she'd expected to walk into house that was as warm as last time as she trudged through the snow.

Bradford had cleaned out the fireplace before leaving and left a nice stack of wood close to it. Claudia knew how to build a fire, so that wasn't a problem. She found a matchbox with three sticks, and immediately she was alert. The match sticks mustn't be wasted.

She arranged the wood-cabin log style, packed kindling, a mixture of bark, dried grass, and newspapers in between the cabin log structure, struck the match, and lit a portion of the newspaper. Soon the fire was going. She added more wood, but it was never as much heat as the day she'd come with Max.

As Claudia straightened from getting the fire going, she realized she'd reached a decision on who to choose. "That was easy." Thinking of something else had given her mind time to come up with a solution.

Feeling good with herself, she walked over to the window and peeked out. The snowfall was now coming down heavily. "The blizzard as advertised," she said out loud.

She could start heading back to the resort now but for the snow. Claudia moved away from the window. She would have to stay until the storm was over.

She took off her jacket, poked the fire, and added some logs to it. She lowered herself onto Bradford's bed and dozed off.

When Claudia opened her eyes, it was pitch black and cold. She had no idea how long she'd slept, but during her slumber, she had wrapped herself up like a mummy. She patted around the bed, looking for her cell phone, then stopped. "Damn." She'd left her phone in her room. She'd remembered where while hiking. Claudia kicked herself for not thinking of a scenario where she couldn't see to get the fire going in the dark. Well, that was what the flashlight on phones was for.

Claudia retraced her steps, found her jacket, and put it back on. She continued feeling her way around, looking for the matchbox. She found it, went over to the fireplace, and looked for newspapers.

"Ouch!" The fire burned to the end of the matchstick and burned Claudia's finger. She dropped it, and the flame died out. Right away, darkness engulfed her. It took a while to get used to the dark again.

Outside, the wind screeched. The house groaned and

creaked with the onslaught. Claudia had the matchbox with her and lit another match. She found the bark and dry leaves and was walking to the fireplace when the stick burned out. That was when Claudia realized that was her last stick.

She searched in the dark, feeling her way around, but couldn't find another matchbox. It was so cold she could barely feel her fingers.

Claudia stopped searching and decided to put her gloves back on—better to conserve heat. In the morning, it would be a lot easier to search with daylight.

She felt her way back to the bed, wrapped herself up, and lay there shivering, afraid she might freeze to death if she dozed off.

47

Max

MAX WAS IN THE LOUNGE NURSING A CUP OF COFFEE AS HE waited for the clock to get to 1 pm. But, unnerved by the whole situation, he couldn't wait around. Five minutes to one, he headed for Claudia's room.

At about this time two days ago, he had been getting ready to leave town and take a job with the CIA that could get him killed. A dangerous job. A way to deal with Claudia instead of putting her through his PTSD. Then just as he was about to leave, she sauntered in, fucked his brains out, and gave him a reason to stay back.

He recalled her exact words from that day: *"Don't you see, Max? We...we're both damaged...We're meant for each other."*

Now he'd just found out that he had two competitors. And this was not high school where it was all rated PG, where the guys carry the girl's books or do her homework. While another is driving her around like a chauffeur and his allowance is at her disposal-her ATM, with no benefits either. This was X rated stuff. Those two guys were tapping the pussy.

Max laughed and shook his head, surprised he wasn't mad that other guys were fucking her. How could a woman with the image of a girl next door have three men eating out of her hand? If she had started off with that plan in mind, to rope together three guys for a reason, he didn't think it would've worked. It seemed like she was a victim as much as he and the rest of the guys were—victims of love.

Claudia's face came to his mind, and just like that, he felt a twitch in his pants, and his cock started to get hard. "There's really something about Claudia," he muttered to himself.

Minutes later, Max walked down the hallway toward her room. He thought he was the first to arrive, but Ron was already there. Max acknowledged him with an upward nod; Ron did the same. They stood in awkward silence.

"Did you knock?" asked Max.

"Not yet." Ron inhaled, then exhaled. "Should I?"

"It's already one. Why not?" Max raised his palms. "Hold on. I hope you don't mind. How…how did you guys discover you liked each other?"

"Me and Claudia?"

Max nodded.

"Oh, she was coaching me on skiing, and I was instructing her on fashion and ballroom dancing."

"Ah, the dance!" Max sighed. "Yes, she mentioned it."

"Hey, Ron! You couldn't let this go, right?" said a voice.

Max and Ron turned and saw Wyatt coming toward them.

"I should have let your ass take off from that cliff, and you wouldn't be here," said Wyatt. "It would have just been between Marine boy here and me." He pointed at Max.

Max wanted to intervene, then thought it was better to hear him out first.

Wyatt exhaled. "Ron, I find a good thing, and you find a way to fuck it up for me because of something that happened ages ago. I know you're trying to get back at me because of your girlfriend. But-"

"She wasn't just my girlfriend, Webb. I was going to marry her!"

Wyatt pointed a finger at Ron. "She was culpable too. Don't blame just me. I'd just won the championship, and every girl wanted a piece of me. If she hadn't offered, I wouldn't have taken. Do you have any idea how hard it is to say no to free, no strings attached pussy thrown at you?" Wyatt paused for effect. "Well, let me tell you, it is extremely hard." He threw open his palms. "I wonder how these celebrities do it. I'm sorry I fucked your girlfriend. Now you've slept with mine, and that makes us even."

Ron shook his head. "She's not your girlfriend."

"Whatever. Can you please forget about Claudia and go cuddle with Riley?"

"Riley is a lesbian…And moreover, I'm in love with Claudia, and she's in love with me."

"Wow, wow, wow," said Max. "Hold your horses, guys. The lady's with me."

Ron and Wyatt looked at each other, then back at Max.

It was a contemptuous look like they knew something he didn't.

"Why don't we put an end to this?" said Wyatt. "Why don't we ask her?"

He rubbed his hands together. "Good idea." He stepped forward and knocked on the door. There was no reply. He knocked again. "Maybe she's not there."

Ron reached into his pocket, and so did Wyatt. They both pulled out their cell phones.

"There it is," said Ron. "Meet me in my room at 1 pm."

Max groaned.

Wyatt tapped his phone. "I got the same message." He looked at Max. "I guess you got the same too."

Max nodded, and this time banged on the door.

Wyatt taped on his screen a few times, and a ringing dial tone came from his speakers. It rang to the end and went to voicemail.

"This is Claudia Kraner. I can't come to the phone right now-"

Wyatt cut it off. "What do you think?"

"I'd say let's give her an hour," said Max. "Maybe she's still working things out in her head."

"So we meet back here?" asked Ron.

Max exhaled. "I'll be at the lounge. Anyone want to join me for a drink?" He glanced from Wyatt to Ron. Neither of them moved. Max shrugged. "Suit yourself." He turned and walked to the lounge.

"I see you're still here," said Paul as he handed Max his coffee. "The power of women."

Max shook his head and reached for his coffee. "Tell me about it." He took his mug and headed to a couch with a good view of the TV. "I'll watch some TV over there."

Max lowered himself on the couch, eyes glued to the TV. He wondered what was going on in Claudia's mind. He wouldn't want to trade places with her right now but wanted to be around her, to help her pick him.

Max had been sitting for about ten minutes, staring at the TV when a shadow passed over him. He looked up. It was Wyatt. Behind him was Ron. Max raised an eyebrow.

Wyatt pointed at the couch.

Max looked away, pursed his lips, and nodded. Both men took their seats, albeit reluctantly.

They sat in silence, glancing at the TV every now and then and taking a sip from their mugs. Time flies when you're having fun, and rather slowly when you're waiting. It seemed like forever before it was two in the afternoon.

Ron threw his palms open. "Shall we?"

Max stood up and looked out the window. "The snow is coming down." He led the way, and they went back to Claudia's room. He knocked several times and got no reply. Then he banged on the door.

The men exchanged glances.

"Maybe it's time we smashed the door," said Wyatt and brought out his cell phone again.

"Should…should we call the police?" asked Ron, rocking back and forth.

Wyatt scoffed. "You don't report a person missing until after twenty-four hours."

"You've been watching too much TV," said Max. "You can report as soon as you feel concerned."

They stood in silence, then Wyatt suddenly started to laugh.

Max eyed him.

"Don't you guys get it?" said Wyatt, shaking his head. "She wanted to get us all together-to figure it out on our own. She never planned to be here."

Max didn't like Wyatt very much, but he might be right.

"I'm going to my room to take a nap," said Wyatt. "I'll be back by five." He walked away.

"You think he's right?" asked Ron.

"I don't know, but by five, if none of us has heard from her, we'll have to escalate our efforts." Max pointed his thumb toward the lounge. "I'll be there." He walked away.

48

Max

MAX FELT A NUDGE ON HIS SHOULDER. HE COULD HEAR THE chopper coming in to evacuate them amid other sounds. Maybe it was the enemy, trying to determine if he was still alive. Max was nudged again, and this time he'd timed it. It was three seconds between the first and second prod.

Max began to count down. The third prod would be the person's last. One thousand and one, one thousand and two, one thousand and-his right hand sprang up as he opened his eyes. He grabbed the wrist, ready to twist and dislocate.

"Ouch, dude!" yelled Wyatt. "What the fuck. Let go." He glared at Max.

Max glared back, then let go. "Sorry. I must have dozed off." The chopper sound and the noise Max heard in his dream were people talking and the Christmas song in the background.

"It's five," said Wyatt, massaging his wrist. "I called Claudia's number but still no answer."

Max sat up and looked around. "Where's Ron?"

"He's outside in the hallway. In case…in case Claudia comes through."

Max reached into his pocket. "All right." He fished out his cell phone, swiped the screen, and tapped an icon.

A female mechanical voice said, "Type in the number you want to locate."

"Readout Claudia's number."

Wyatt pulled out his phone, tapped on the screen, and read out Claudia's number.

Max tapped in the number and hit enter. The hourglass icon spun around for a few seconds and then stopped. A map came up with a green teardrop showing the location of the phone. Max felt the hairs at the nape of his neck rise. "She's here," he said in a low voice.

"What?" asked Wyatt.

Max turned the phone to Wyatt.

Wyatt's eyes widened as he looked at the phone. "She's here at the resort?" He looked up at Max. "Dude, you had this app on your phone, and you didn't think you should check until four hours later?"

Max held his gaze. "Haven't you ever heard of privacy? Maybe that's how she wanted it." Max stabbed a finger at Wyatt. "Wasn't that what you suggested?" He stood up.

Wyatt got closer, into his face. "If anything happens to Claudia…by God…I'll…I'll…" His voice trailed off. He looked like he was going to cry.

Max looked away. He felt like he was back in the deserts of Afghanistan, anticipating a Taliban attack. He'd seen men lose their nerve in the face of danger. "Come, we have to get into her room. I'll get a spare key from the office."

"Hey, what happened?" asked Ron as soon as they stepped into the hallway. His face turned pale.

Wyatt saw Ron and his bluster returned. "Marine boy has a phone locater app on his cell. It says Claudia's phone is here - we want to go get a spare key."

"My God," said Ron. "What if she's hurt in her room? We might be too late already." He ran down the hall toward Claudia's room.

Wyatt and Max ran after him.

Ron got there and threw his shoulder into the door. He fell back as if the door had pushed him back.

Wyatt took a running leap and kicked the door. He too, ended up on the floor beside Ron. Ron scrambled to his feet, ready to take another shot at the door.

"Hold it," said Max. "There's a trick to kicking down doors." He stepped back, raised his right foot, his dominant leg, and planted a solid kick just above the door handle. There was a loud crack, and the door flew open.

Max stepped in; the faint smell of Claudia's perfume engulfed him. "Claudia!"

Ron opened the bathroom door and stepped in. He came out and shook his head.

Max's heart thumped in his chest as he walked to the side of the bed close to the wall. He didn't want to see her lying on the floor.

Wyatt walked to the other side of the bed.

Max exhaled. She wasn't there.

"She's not here," said Ron and ran his hand over his chin. "Where could she be?"

"Just her clothes in here," said Wyatt, looking into her closet.

Max pulled out his phone again. "But the phone locater said she's in this address." He called her number.

A phone started to ring by the bed. It was a muffled sound.

Max picked up the bed cover and pulled away. No phone.

"Under the bed," blurted Wyatt, and dove for the floor.

Max dropped to the floor and looked under the bed too. Empty. But the phone continued to ring.

Ron walked over to the drawer beside the bed and pulled it open. The muffled ringing got louder. "It's here! Her cell is here." He picked up the phone. "Jesus, she left without her phone."

"Her text to me was around 12:30 pm," said Max. "And it's now almost 6 pm. That's a long time. We must ask people if they saw her or the last time they did. Let's hit the parking lot and see if her car is there."

"What about the door?" asked Ron as they left Claudia's room.

"Fuck the door," said Wyatt.

Max shut the door as best as he could. "We'll deal with it later. I think there's a party going on there." He pointed at the lounge. "Wyatt, you want to check it out in case she's there?"

"Okay. If she's not there, I'll meet you guys outside."

Max and Ron came outside and stopped in their tracks.

"Shit," said Max. The parking lot was filled with cars, and each car had a decent coating of snow on it. "She drives a Honda Accord. Apart from SUVs, we need to brush snow off most of the cars."

Ron pointed at a set of cars covered in snow closest to the building. "Let's start over there. She normally parks there."

"I'll grab a brush from my car," said Max. "I think I have a spare one."

Luckily, it was dry snow, easily shoved off with the sweep of a hand. They brushed snow from a lot of cars. As they brushed off the snow, more fell. They found a few Honda Accords, but they weren't Claudia's.

"You think she went home?" asked Ron. "Most people

would go home when they need to think. You know, a familiar place."

That was a possibility, thought Max.

Wyatt nodded. "Yeah. Let's try that."

Ron and Wyatt turned to Max.

Max sighed. "It falls on the local lover boy to lead the way. We'll use my truck. I know her aunt is staying there now."

By the time they passed through Main Street, the snow was coming down continuously, getting heavier and heavier. By the time they got to Claudia's house, it was late, and her aunt was already in bed.

When Aunt Sam came to the door after they rang the bell the third time, she stared at the three men and said, "Santa must have made a mistake. I only asked for one hunk for Christmas."

The guys laughed and introduced themselves.

"Please call me Sam."

Max had become something of their spokesman. He apologized for disturbing her Christmas Eve and said they thought they'd come and surprise Claudia with a visit.

"Don't worry," said Aunt Sam. "You'll find her. So, which one of you is Claudia's boyfriend?"

Crickets.

"My goodness."

Max cleared his throat. "Umm...Sam, when was the last time you saw Claudia?"

Sam thought for a moment. "Yes, some days ago. She came in late at night and left early in the morning. She said she was going hiking. Yes, to Fox Run with Steel."

Max hit his forehead with his palm. "Of course!" He grabbed Aunt Sam and spun her around. "Merry Christmas!"

"What's this Fox Run?" asked Ron, excitement in his voice.

"I think I know where she went," said Max, speaking fast as they headed to his truck and piled in.

Wyatt let out a huge sigh of relief. "Thank goodness. How far of a drive is this place?"

"How much of a hike," said Max.

Ron raised his hands. "We'll be hiking?"

"Yes, and it's about thirty minutes. But considering the weather, maybe an additional hour."

"How sure are you she's there?" asked Ron.

"Probably 99.99 percent," said Max. "It's the kind of place you go for solitude. But not in weather like this."

"I'm coming," said Wyatt.

"Count me in," said Ron.

Max nodded. "Okay. We'll need gear. We must dress warm-snowshoes, thermal underwear, the whole works. There's a blizzard out there, and we need to be prepared. We'll borrow what we need from the resort's shed."

They drove on in silence, every man to his own thought.

"It's going to be risky, guys," said Max as the wiper created a screeching sound as it brushed snow off the wind- shield. "You don't have to come."

Wyatt and Ron said nothing. By the time they picked up the gear from the shed and drove up to Fox Run Ridge, it was Christmas Day.

Max drove into the Fox Run parking. A car completely buried in snow was parked there. His heart hammered in his chest. "The good thing is there's a car here, and it could be Claudia's. We'll have to make sure she's not inside."

Ron brushed off the back. "It's a Honda!"

Max unzipped his backpack, brought out a shovel, and cleaned around the vehicle. It was Claudia's car, all right.

Wyatt shined the flashlight in. It was empty. "What next?"

"We climb up," said Max. "There seems to be more snow up here. Probably more in the cabin. Guys, I know we all feel the same for Claudia and want her for ourselves alone. But we must work together. Otherwise, we might be too late. I hope she made it to the cabin before this storm started. I've been up this mountain many times, although not in these conditions. All I ask is you listen to me and-"

"Dude, I looked you up. You're like Rambo," said Wyatt. "What if you kill Ron and me up there and have Claudia all to yourself?"

Max shook his head. "I have skills, but we need speed. Three guys can shovel faster than one. Listen, Claudia is already hurting from losing her mother. What do you think will happen to her state of mind if she believes she is responsible for any of us dying?"

"Show me how to use the snowshoes," said Ron.

49

Claudia

CLAUDIA HAD NEVER BEEN THIS COLD IN HER LIFE. SHE'D been cold before, but always for a limited period, like taking the trash out early in the morning when the thermometer was in the teens with the wind chill dragging it down to single digits. Or walking from one building to another, waiting for the bus or train. Then she'd felt cold, but Claudia had known it was only for a limited period. She would get to her destination and be enveloped by warmth. Not tonight. There was no respite.

The cold was unrelenting. Claudia's fingers, toes, ears, and nose were so cold it hurt. What was she going to do? This was not the time to do jumping jacks to keep warm.

She thought of the day she'd come with Max. It was cold outside, but it had been so warm inside the cabin. Claudia's mind drifted to how she'd ended up here, about to freeze to death.

Was anyone looking for her? If only she had her phone

with her. Claudia wanted to laugh at the irony of what was happening. She was a victim of her own making. She'd fallen in love with three men and trying to decide who to choose had landed her in this predicament.

She was going to freeze to death. Claudia didn't want to be negative, but it was hard not to. Her pulse started to race as she saw a ray of hope. She'd told her boys to meet her in her room, inadvertently, at the same time. Maybe they'd all met up in her room and now realized something was wrong.

Only Max knew she was aware of the cabin in the mountain, but it might not occur to him that she would come here. And even if he did, he would think she wanted privacy. Max was a decent man and would give her time to sort through her thoughts. Her newfound hope faded just as it had come to her.

Claudia's head jerked as the door and windows rattled. Was it just the wind? Was there something sinister out there? Claudia shivered both from the cold and fear. It was pitch black outside; the snow was really coming down, blocking out any light from the moon. The worst thing that could happen to her was a cave-in.

Where was that sunrise? She'd lost track of time. Something she could have easily looked up on her phone, but she didn't have it. At least with daylight, she could see what she was dealing with.

Just yesterday, she was as happy as could be. Now she was battling with sadness. What a difference less than twenty-four hours could make. Why her?

Her feelings of sadness always navigated back to her mother. Was she being punished for her mother's death? It was a guilt she'd always carried and had found a way to deal with it. But now she'd talked about it. Were their forces angry with her? Suddenly something occurred to Claudia. She'd always blamed herself for what happened, but she'd never asked her mother for forgiveness.

Claudia drifted in and out of consciousness. *Please don't sleep, please don't sleep.* She was scared that once she closed her eyes, she wouldn't wake up again. She was going to die anyway. A sob escaped her throat. "Mom, please forgive me. If I knew I was sending you to your death, I would never have thrown a tantrum. You were the best mother ever, and every day I've had to live with what I did. I love you and miss you."

It had been fourteen years since her mother had died. Still, the only image that came to Claudia's mind was the image of her mother's face, tight-lipped, wearing a light black winter jacket grabbing her handbag and leaving the house. She sobbed, her tears forming a crust on her eyes from the cold.

Claudia must have fallen asleep because she awoke to a bright image of her mother suspended in the air smiling at her.

"Don't blame yourself, Claudia," said the image. "You were only a child. The accident wasn't your fault. Things do happen, and there's nothing for me to forgive. But I want you to forgive yourself. Now rest, my dear child."

Claudia smiled. A calmness she'd never experienced before took over her body, and she drifted away.

50

Claudia

THE HEAT WAS INTENSE. IF THIS WAS HELL, CLAUDIA NEVER wanted to be any other place. Was her mother here? Probably not. She would be in heaven.

The brightness behind her closed eyelids forced her to keep them that way. She was happy and, at the same time, scared. What would she see when she opened her eyes?

Claudia used her other senses. She became aware of the crackling fire, the smell of wood smoke, sweat, and faint animal fat. They were all familiar.

She'd tried to open her eyes, but the brightness behind her eyelids was so intense she dared not. She'd read Dante's *Inferno* somewhere and wondered what level of hell she was at right now.

Claudia heard voices. *What language was spoken in hell?* Dante Alighieri, the author of *Divine Comedy*, was from Florence, and Claudia thought they should be speaking Italian. But they seemed to be speaking English. But then, she didn't think that hell would discriminate against people based on their nationality.

"Add more wood to the fire!" a voice barked.

The voice sounded far away. A voice used to issuing orders and having them carried out. But it was familiar too. Moments later, Claudia heard a *clunk clunk clunk* sound. She presumed logs of wood were tossed into the fire.

"Ron…Wyatt, thanks so much for not letting me do this alone. I didn't expect we'd have to literally dig our way through the snow to get to the cabin."

"Come on, Max, there's no way in hell we would have let you do that. Claudia is our girl too."

That was Wyatt's voice. Claudia put the picture together, and her heart leaped with joy. Her boys had come for her.

"Who's crazy enough to live up here without electricity, anyway?" said Ron.

Max chuckled. "His name is Bradford. The old timer loves it just the way it is."

Ron continued. "If it wasn't for that Swiss knife backpack of yours, it would have been impossible to make it here on time."

"Phew," said Wyatt. "Night vision goggles, battery-powered saw, and the telescopic shovel. You should hook me up with one, Max."

"Will do. Don't forget the manpower, guys," said Max. "There's no way one person could have cleared all that snow in record time. The doors and windows were completely snowed in. A lot is achieved when people work as a team. We had the same objective-Claudia."

Claudia was thawed and warmed.

She opened her eye a slit, saw them, and shut it right away. Her heart thundered in her chest. She'd gone from nearly freezing to death to being consumed by internal heat.

They had really came for her. She'd never been so embarrassed in her life. Three grown men wanting her.

"She's awake! She's awake," said Ron.

Max and Wyatt stopped what they were doing. The three of them gathered around her.

Claudia smiled and looked down at her hands. "Hello."

"Hello back," said Max. "You had us all worried. How do you feel? It's nice and warm now. Do you want a drink?" He squeezed her shoulder. "Stay right there, let me see what I have in my backpack."

"Dance partner," said Ron. "You should have told us we were coming for a game of hide and seek when you invited us to your room."

Wyatt nudged Ron on the shoulder. "Come on Ron, give her a break. She didn't know."

Claudia's eyes widened. "You...you guys are now friends?"

Wyatt winked. "You brought us together, remember...in your room?"

Heat rushed to Claudia's cheeks, and she covered her face with her hands. This was going to take getting used to.

Max passed a small plastic cup to her. "Here. That should warm you up from the inside."

Max was right. The vodka burned its way through her system. Claudia sat up, the alcohol was overheating her. She removed the blankets covering her and took off her jacket. She took a deep breath and exhaled through her mouth. Underneath, she had on a thick sweater. She took that off too, stripping down basically to her long-sleeved thermal underwear and leggings. "It's so nice here now."

"Oh, it was a freezer when we got here," said Wyatt.

"I ran out of matches. It was dark, and I didn't have my phone. I forgot it in my room."

Ron nodded. "That makes sense. By the way, Merry Christmas, Claudia."

Claudia's face brightened. "That's true, Merry Christmas. You're like the three wise men bearing gifts."

Max smiled. "Three wise men sounds cool. Okay, we three wise men, although some would call us foolish, braved almost two hours of hiking in blizzard conditions to get to you, to bring you Christmas tidings. We bonded along the way and have become thick as thieves." Max took a deep breath and exhaled. "Now, Claudia Kraner, the moment of truth has arrived. You have no lifeline. You cannot call a friend and or poll the audience. The billion-dollar question is － "

"Drum roll," said Wyatt and beat out a beat on his thigh.

"All right, Ms. Kraner, which one of these wise men do you pick?"

Claudia's breath caught. She wasn't ready for this type of life-changing decision-making. "I need to pee."

They all stared at her as if she was speaking a foreign language.

"I need to go. Tinkle?"

"Yes right," said Wyatt. "Max, where is the bathroom in this off-grid cabin?"

Max sighed, shaking his head. "It's outside, but the door is buried by at least six feet of snow. Don't worry, love, I'll find you a pot to piss in."

Ron threw back his head and laughed. "A pot to piss in."

Max did find her a pot. And as she did her business, she wondered the best way to present her answer. She'd already made up her mind, but how would they take it? There was no other way but to lay it out there. She would have to try. The worst that could happen would be a no. She walked back to them.

Wyatt started the drum roll for the second time.

A nervous smile danced on Claudia's lips. She couldn't make eye contact with any of them, and it was getting increasingly hot. "I can't pick - I want you all." She kissed Max, then Ron and finally kissed Wyatt. She went and sat on the bed, looking at them while twiddling her thumbs.

The three of them stared at her with incredulity in their eyes. Finally, Max broke the spell.

"One moment," he said, motioning for the guys to come together in a huddle.

Claudia watched as they talked. Once in a while, one of them would turn around and look at her as if they were the opposing team in the TV game show *Family Feud*.

Her heart hammered in her chest. Was she asking for too much? Could she just deceive them and hang out with them behind each other's backs? After what seemed like an eternity, they turned to face her.

Ron stepped forward. "On behalf of the three wise men, your wish is our command!"

EPILOGUE

CLAUDIA *(NEW YEARS Eve)*

CLAUDIA, MAX, WYATT, AND RON WERE BACK IN THE OFF-grid cabin. It had been six days since that Christmas morning that her three wise men showed up bearing gifts and saved her from freezing to death.

Bradford wasn't coming back until the second week of January, so they decided to usher in the New Year in the cabin. They brought their own food, drinks, and portable entertainment.

They sat on Bradford's bed, sipping drinks from plastic cups with Ron's iPad propped up on books in front of them. They watched Ryan Seacrest host the ball drop at Times Square.

Max had stuck the champagne bottle in the snow outside the door to keep it cool. Champagne flutes already sat on a tray, waiting for the ball to drop. The bottles of rum, Coke, and orange juice they were already drinking from were standing on the floor beside the tray. The plan was to relax and drink all the booze.

Because it had been so cold when they came in, the boys had made a massive fire, and now it was hot in the cabin.

"I can remove some logs," volunteered Max.

"No," said Claudia. "I can't forget that night. And there's a nice feeling of knowing it's freezing outside and you're toasty with barely anything on just a few feet away."

"Tempting faith," said Ron from his vantage point in the middle of the bed.

Claudia had peeled off her clothes as it got hotter and was down to a large, borrowed T-shirt from Max and her underwear. Her boys were mostly in T-shirts and pants.

A small square Bluetooth speaker delivered sound. Music, remarks, and commentary came through the iPad. The sound was so clear they could've been in Times Square themselves.

For about thirty minutes now, they'd been sitting on the bed drinking, eating finger food, and commenting about the celebrities. They went back and forth on musical groups, weighing in on their performances. Every now and then, the camera would pull away and show a country that had already celebrated the New Year panning through happy smiling faces, fireworks displays, and people celebrating. In one brief scene that must have caught the cameraman off guard, a woman raised her T-shirt and flashed her boobs, screaming *Happy New Year!* at the top of her lungs.

Three seconds later, Ron looked at Claudia and Wyatt on his right, then turned to the other side to look at Wyatt. "Did you guys see those tits, or were my eyes playing tricks on me?"

"Saw it," said Wyatt. "But the best is right here beside me."

It took a second for Claudia to realize what he meant.

Heat rushed through her. She walked over to the drinks on the floor, bent down, and topped her cup with rum.

Claudia took a big gulp of her drink and stole a look at Ron and Max as she walked back to her place beside Wyatt. *My goodness!* She noticed the huge bulges in her boys' pants. She must have given them an eyeful when she bent down to get her drink.

She flopped down beside Wyatt and eyed the bulge in his pants. She had to investigate; it could be a pregnant gerbil lurking in there. Laughter bubbled out of her at her own joke. It was the rum taking over. Claudia took another sip and placed her cup on the floor.

Eyes straight ahead, staring at the screen, Claudia put her hand under Wyatt's T-shirt, flat against his stomach. She slid down into his pants, under his boxers. She grabbed his cock and squeezed.

Wyatt threw his head back, and his finger traced a path under Claudia's borrowed T-shirt. He made his way into her panties, caressed the hair on her mound, then slid a finger into her.

Claudia's breath hitched as jolts of pleasure traveled through her body. She was wet and ready. Claudia turned to Wyatt and whispered, "Take it off."

Wyatt withdrew his finger from her pussy and pulled his pants and boxers to his ankles. His cock sprang free. She could have said, *Please pass me the popcorn.* His eyes never left the iPad screen.

Claudia straddled him, shifted her panties, positioned his bare cock, and lowered herself onto him.

Wyatt blew air out of his lips as she slid down all the way. He sucked her nipples one after the other through her T-shirt, leaving wet spots.

A jolt of pleasure started from her breasts and sent waves through her, stealing her breath.

His palms cupped her ass. That feeling alone caused her sex to contract around him.

Claudia rode him slowly, squeezing as she went up and down.

She stared into Wyatt's eyes as if casting a spell on him. Their eyes remained on each other with his mouth moving each time she squeezed him deep inside her.

Claudia felt his hands on her ass tighten, and a moan escaped him. A surge of excitement raced through her, but she didn't want to come, not just yet.

She had a plan and put it to work right away. She stopped moving and squeezed Wyatt's cock tighter. Wyatt gasped, his breathing came in heaves. Thighs shaking, he buried his face on Claudia's shoulder as a powerful orgasm tore through him.

When he stopped shaking and released his tight grip on her ass, Claudia got up, took off her panties, and moved over to Ron. There was a look of confusion and excitement on his face. Claudia kneeled in front of him, unzipped his jeans, and pulled out his drpping cock. She wrapped her lips around his knob, tasting him. Then she pulled his pants down to his ankles.

Claudia got up, took his cock in her hands, straddled him, and impaled herself. She ignored the fact she still had Wyatt's juices inside her. He slid in effortlessly, throwing his head back as if he'd finally gotten what he'd been waiting for.

When Ron opened his eyes and looked at hers, their eyes remained glued to each other. Ron was in a hurry, driven by pleasure. He wanted to come right away. He grabbed Claudia's ass and heaved her up and down, and he ground her clit against him by moving her ass back and forth.

Claudia whimpered. The pleasure was too much. If he

continued that, she would come. Claudia grabbed his hands and placed them flat on the bed. She fixed her eyes on him, then squeezed him just as she had done to Wyatt.

"Oh, God" shot out of Ron's lips.

Claudia rode him with the same deliberate rhythm she'd used on Wyatt, her eyes never leaving his. What she felt inside was deeper than sex. Claudia's job was to satisfy the boys in her life.

Ron's breathing came in gasps. He was ready to explode. The fact that he was responding to what she was doing to him almost tipped her over.

But not quite. Claudia had a plan in her mind.

She turned to look at Max and gasped. His pants were already off. He had his cock in his hands, stroking it, sliding his hands up and down his shaft.

Claudia felt encouraged. Her guys were not bothered by sharing her, taking turns one after the other. Whatever happened on Christmas Day as they trudged through the snow to rescue her must have been profound. Ron and Wyatt had already shared her, and now Max was on board.

Ron shuddered, a deep growl poured out of him, and he came inside Claudia.

"About time," muttered Max. He extended his hand like he was in a relay race, ready to grab the baton. He wrapped his arm around Claudia's butt and guided her to him.

Claudia turned to face him, but he spun her around to face the iPad, and she understood. Cowgirl style, she lowered herself on him.

Max let out a satisfied moan as she sheathed him with her warmth. He raised Claudia's shirt and planted wet kisses on her bare back. Max cupped her breasts from behind and hefted them in each palm, letting out a satisfied groan. He rolled her nipples with his fingers, eliciting a moan from Claudia. With her nipples hard as nails, he headed south.

Claudia felt his fingers approach her crotch from both sides. As she raised herself up and down his cock, Max's fingers worked on her clit-side to side, up and down like a shoe shiner buffing her leather. "My goodness," blurted Claudia. "Too much...too soon."

Beside them, Ron and Wyatt watched, breathing hard.

Time after time, Claudia rose and slammed down on him, filling the room with the sound of sex.

Loud moans rushed out of her, but she didn't care. She'd given herself permission to satisfy her boys and enjoy all the sensations that would lead up to her orgasm. She hadn't chosen Max for any reason to be the last one. That was the order they sat on the bed.

Max placed Claudia on her back, grabbed her ankles, and adjusted his hips until his cock nudged her core. He pushed in, then pulled out and plunged in again.

He went faster and harder, and Claudia felt her orgasm rushing toward her. It took a lot of effort on her part. She didn't want him to stop fucking her. But she placed a hand flat on Max's stomach, and he stopped.

"What is it?" asked Max, breathless.

"Nothing," said Claudia, her whole body shaking. She had to claim him like she'd claimed the others, her on top, milking his cock. He could have her any other way he wanted after this.

Max, used to giving orders, this time followed her command. He sat back on the bed. His cock, red and angry, pulsed in the air.

This was her call. Claudia straddled him.

Max moaned. "Oh yes, I need that."

She would fuck him as fast or slow as she wanted. She

worked her hips-back and forth, side to side, grinding down each time she made contact with his body. Claudia tilted to her right and moaned. She'd found the right angle for maximum sensation and rode him hard. Claudia's orgasm came quickly. It grabbed her, causing her whole body to go tense.

Max wrapped his hands around her as she reveled in the throes of ecstasy. Moments later, he grunted and said, "Oh shit" as his own climax grabbed him, and he flooded her pussy.

They held each other, out of breath.

In the background, Claudia heard the countdown to New Years start as she squeezed Max's cock, milking the last drop. She kissed Max, then got off him. Their climax was perfect timing. New Year, new beginnings with her wise men, thought Claudia, as their combined sex trickled down her inner thigh.

Wyatt got up, opened the door, and grabbed the champagne bottle, letting in a gust of cold air. He filled the flutes quickly.

Max pulled up his pants and buttoned them. He grabbed a glass of champagne from Wyatt.

Everyone had a drink in hand. All four of them faced the iPad and started to count down with the folks on TV.

"Five, four, three, two, one. Happy New Year!!"

On the screen, the crystal ball came down.

They all clinked glasses. "CHEERS!"

THE END!

JOIN MY NEWSLETTER

Want to receive the latest information on my upcoming novels and receive a FREE book? Sign up for my free author newsletter by clicking on Brie Wilds Newsletter or visit www.briewilds.com

ALSO BY BRIE WILDS

BB Follow on BookBub

Follow me on BookBub to learn more

ABOUT THE AUTHOR

Brie Wilds is the author of The Neighbor Who Stole Christmas, Book 1 of the Mountain Peak Series. She writes steamy, romance stories, about men and women, and their amazing and unique journey to finding happily ever after.